the DARK SIDE

the DARK SIDE

SATHYA SARAN

An imprint of Manjul Books

First published in India by Anthem,
an imprint of:

Manjul Books Pvt. Ltd.
10, Nishat Colony, Bhopal, INDIA - 462 003
Phone : +91-755-4240340, Fax : +91-755-2736919
E-mail : manjul@manjulindia.com
Website : www.manjulindia.com

First published by Manjul Books - 2007

First published in 1996 as *The Night Train and Other Stories*. Some new stories have been added, while some have been removed.

Copyright © Sathya Saran.

This is entirely a work of fiction. The names, characters and incidents portrayed in it are the work of the author's imagination. Any resemblance to actual persons, living or dead, is entirely coincidental.

ISBN-13   978 - 81 - 89631 - 26 - 0
ISBN-10   81 - 89631 - 26 - 8

Printed & bound in India by
Thomson Press (India) Ltd., New Delhi, INDIA

All rights reserved. No part of this publication may be reproduced, stored in or introduced into a retrieval system, or transmitted, in any form, or by any means (electronic, mechanical, photocopying, recording or otherwise) without the prior written permission of the publisher. Any person who does any unauthorized act in relation to this publication may be liable to criminal prosecution and civil claims for damages.

Contents

Foreword	i
Preface	iii
1. A Practical Joke	5
2. Shock Treatment	13
3. Night Train to Glasgow	25
4. Nightwatch	35
5. Exchange Counter	45
6. I Spy	53
7. The Old Man and the Tree	61
8. A Bicycle for Two	67
9. Beyond the Looking Glass	97
10. Diwali Promise	105
11. Smoke Rings	111
12. Last Supper	121
13. A Toothful Tale	127
14. A Sunday Evening	133
15. After the Bomb	139

CONTENTS

16. Rendezvous	155
17. Too Late for Amends	161
18. The Seven-Cornered Table	167
19. Tram Rider	183
20. The Lost Note	189
21. A Good Wife	197

FOREWORD

WHEN THIS COLLECTION was first published as *Night Train and Other Stories,* stories about the surreal were not the norm in Indian publishing, except for one or two very well-known exceptions.

Despite this, *Night Train and Other Stories* was hugely enjoyed by everyone who read it, and the hardcover collection of short stories went into a second print run.

This collection contains most of the stories of that volume, with a few brand new ones added.

It's a book you can take on a train journey, or read on a rainy day, or on one of those lovely days when your time is your own. It is meant to be an escape from the mundane, from routine.

I am grateful to Manjul Books for their readiness to bring back into print these stories that had all but vanished from the bookstores, though some still linger in people's memories.

Sathya Saran

PREFACE

EACH OF THESE stories wrote itself. The idea would seize me – the germ of an idea, actually – and I would sit down, pen in hand, to write. And before I could get up, the story would write itself down, word after word, line after line, till the very end.

The stories in this book fall into two main categories – the more obvious one is the group that deals with the surreal. Not really the supernatural, though there are elements of that in some stories, but the surreal, which could be something beyond the real, or it could be the mind itself, bending in ways not normally bent, to experience that which is not normally experienced.

The other group deals with real emotions in daily life, felt by people who have, so to say, been picked up from their business of daily living, to be put under a microscope and be examined for what they feel and think and experience. Many of these stories are based on a sentence or a snatch of a mood I have noticed in a friend, an acquaintance, or as in the case of the 'Last Supper' – a celebrity director of quality films.

The stories span many years of writing – through the 1980s and 90s and many of them have been published in magazines (*Debonair, Imprint, Femina, Science Today,*

The Illustrated Weekly) and newspapers. The rest of them remained unpublished mainly because, some day, I hoped this book would happen. Also, because in the burgeoning business of journal publishing, there are few really worthy vehicles for a different kind of short story. I'm not saying this with pride in my work, but in despair over the literary scene. Only one story, 'A Bicycle for Two' was written to order. It was to be the base for Shekhar Kapur's 'Time Machine,' and I was told to play around with two elements from 'Back to the Future' – a lost mother and a son who finds her in the past. The story in this book was never made into a film – but I enjoyed writing it anyway.

In a life where writing could easily become a chore, and where words are the currency of one's profession, the ability to pen a story is a blessing. It lifts one away from the petty cares of editing and compiling and the pressures of deadlines, to a realm where one can float free without fear of public disapproval or censorship, of expectation of praise and applause.

Yet, when I present this book, I have bound myself down to all that the writing of these stories freed me from. Because a writer is a performer, too, and needs her performance to be noticed and judged, accepted and applauded. If in these stories there is even one that makes every reader sit up and read closely, shutting out the rest of the world, leaving behind the milk on the boil, the day's accounts and ignoring the telephone or the door bell, I will be vindicated. That will be my applause and to that applause, though it may never reach my ears, I raise my glass of hope.

Sathya Saran

1
A PRACTICAL JOKE

LAKSHMI AKKA SAW the ghost three months after Tamba Mama's death. Of course, we were all upset when Mama died. He collapsed suddenly just as he was getting into the plane at the Kennedy airport and there was no reason for his ghost to haunt us, but Lakshmi Akka saw it all the same. Lakshmi Akka was that kind of a person.

Well, it was Akka's dramatic recounting of her encounters with the ghost that started it all. At least that is how Thambi got hold of the idea. And once Thambi gets an idea, it is as good as done. "It just stood there and looked at me," Akka said, pointing to the green foliage of the mango tree that hung outside the verandah. The verandah is at least 25 feet above the ground, you know how these old houses are, with high ceilings and lots of trees all around, and it would have needed much balancing on the ghost's part to stand where Akka said it did, but we heard her out. "I was studying, and suddenly there was a swishing sound, and when I looked up, Mama was there. Standing and looking at me, what big eyes he had…" She stopped, overcome with the memory. In spite of ourselves, and our knowledge of Akka's capacity to turn ropes into snakes, we were impressed.

Anyway, that night, Thambi hatched his plot. Now, if you know our family, you must know that Thambi and Pratibha are eternally at loggerheads. Actually, they are fond of each other, but the fact that they live in different cities, and get to meet only once a year during the summer vacations, is why they fight all the time. Unlike Lakshmi Akka, who lives in Madras, Thambi lives in Bombay and Pratibha in Ahmedabad, and they come to Madras when their respective parents get together under the ancestral roof, once a year. Pratibha is boisterous and dominating. I prefer Lakshmi Akka any day, and so I was happy when I heard Thambi's plan.

"You keep out of this," he said to me. "One hint from you about this, and I'll wring your scrawny neck." He looked as if he would do it too, though I knew he wouldn't. I was the youngest in that group of cousins, that year. The other cousin, Chitra, who is my age, had gone off to Kashmir, and so I was forced to tag on to the others. They tried their best to keep me out of things, and only a week ago, I had been allowed to join the group on tolerance, since I had them all at my mercy. I had seen Thambi teaching Pratibha to smoke, and I told them I would tell Mummy about it. They never asked me to leave them alone, after that. In fact, Pratibha even suggested I come along with them to an adult movie, and lent me her heels to look grown up in. Now I take care to stand guard whenever Pratibha and Thambi are smoking. It wouldn't do for me if they got caught at it.

Anyway, as I was saying, Thambi hatched his plan beautifully. He was going to conjure up the ghost again, for Pratibha's benefit, to teach her once and for all, who had the upper hand in that relationship.

The scene of the drama was the first floor bathroom. If you have seen our bathroom, you will know why there could have been no better setting.

In the olden days, when my grandfather first built the house, the upper bathroom, which he personally used, was something of a marvel. It was tiled in sparkling white squares, and had a huge tub to slosh about in. To provide the hot and cold water, there was a special structure made of pipes that stood a semicircle about six feet high, with one of the pipes ending in a shower. The other end of the pipe ran into the wall to emerge as hot and cold water taps elsewhere in the room. Quite a structure, actually.

But time and the fact that the bathroom floor had begun to seep had made the bathroom unusable. We all had our baths downstairs, and the upper floor bathroom was only there for emergencies... at night. Normally, we preferred not to use it anyway, and crept down the stairs. The moonlight, when it shone on the verandah, gave the tiled bathroom a ghostly glitter, and the semicircle of pipes seemed menacing, like an iron ghost ready to fold you in its steely embrace.

In short, we avoided the bathroom. Except Pratibha that is. She would walk up to it every night, whistling loudly to prove she was not afraid, and emerge with wet face, to prove she had indeed turned on the squeaky tap over the wash basin, and washed her face. "Scaredy cats," she would say looking at us, and smile, while Thambi fumed.

What better site for the recreation of the ghost? The plan was perfect. "I'll wrap myself in a sheet and stand behind the door, and push it shut after Pratibha. Then, when she opens her eyes after washing the soap off her face, I shall materialise," Thambi said. "The door will be shut. What fun," Lakshmi giggled, and I could hardly stand

A PRACTICAL JOKE

for the excitement.

Thursday night was fixed for the joke. Two nights away. We spent Wednesday afternoon oiling the door hinges so they would not creak when Thambi shut the door; and stole a bed sheet from the linen cupboard. We painted two eyes on it with dhobi ink. And we were ready.

Thursday night came. A moonlit night, cool and clear, despite the summer month. On moonlit nights, the moonlight filters through the blue panes of the verandah windows and falls pale and blue on the floor just outside the bathroom door. To my eyes, it looked spooky, but then, I have always found it easy to scare myself. Even from the evening, I could not contain my excitement. Thambi kept giving me stern warning looks across the room, as we sat on the floor of the kitchen eating dinner. It would not do for any of the elders to suspect we were up to anything, his look said. As for Pratibha, there was no danger of her noticing. As usual, she was engrossed in a book, which she insisted on reading at dinner and lunch time every day despite all orders to the contrary.

We washed our hands and sat around for a little while as usual, making polite conversation with the elders. God, I thought, will it never be time to go up?

It was, soon enough. We wended our way upstairs. "Oh, I am so sleepy today," Thambi said loudly, with a huge yawn. Lakshmi Akka nudged me, and I almost giggled loudly. Pratibha was however at the head of the stairs, and did not hear me, as she was too busy telling Thambi what a lazy bug he was.

We flopped down on our beds on the floor, and made desultory conversation, as Thambi continued to pretend sleep, and I was afraid of saying something wrong. "Lights out," said Lakshmi Akka, and switched off the light.

Pratibha made no murmur of protest. Neither did she get up to wash her face. The whole plan was going to flop because Pratibha was feeling lazy tonight. What a waste of excitement!

Thambi had begun to snore, when Pratibha sat up with a start. "My God, I must be mad, I forgot to wash my face..." she said, and started for the bathroom. She had barely turned the corner, when Thambi jumped up, and pulled the sheet out from under his pillow. I sat up too. "Ssh, you stay put, or you will giggle and spoil everything. You and Lakshmi stay put. Anyway, someone will have to snore, or she will wonder what happened to my sleep," he added, pushing my head firmly down into the pillow. I shut my eyes, and began snoring loudly. Thambi disappeared towards the bathroom with the sheet still wrapped up on his arm.

AAAAH! Ammma... the scream was loud, yet not piercing. Pratibha's voice can make a field cannon blush, but fear had choked its full force. I jumped up from Thambi's bed, switched on the lights and stood waiting to see her. She came rushing out from the room nearest the verandah. Her eyes staring, her mouth still open after her scream. "I saw him... He was there, he almost touched me..." she whispered, then collapsed in a heap on the bed. Before I could tell her what the truth was, and that it was only Thambi, she broke into loud sobs. Uncontrollable terrible sobs of shock... Lakshmi Akka tried to console her, and I set off to look for our ghost. Thambi was nowhere to be found. "Thambi," I whispered, "Come out, she's crying, you tell her it was a joke." No response. "Thambi," I said, "Come out, suppose she falls sick or something..."

I wandered into the bathroom, crossing the blue moonlight across the verandah floor. The door was open,

A PRACTICAL JOKE

and Thambi stood behind the shower, the sheet half open in his hands. "What the hell are you doing here? She'll come any minute now, go away," he whispered.

"What?" I asked, confused. Thambi can sometimes carry a joke too far. "Come on Thambi, she's crying in fright, you better console her."

Thambi's mouth fell, he stared at me. "What are you talking about?" he asked. "She was still getting her cream and soap out of the verandah cupboard when I slipped in here. She hasn't even been into the bathroom. And I have not yet scared her!"

2

SHOCK TREATMENT

JANUARY 1

Today I, T. N. Raman, have begun to see. The damage done to my life almost thirty years ago due to a blow I received on my head in a bus accident has at last been rectified. Kind of Dr. V. to suggest my name out of turn for the transplant, but he knows I am single and rich enough to return the favour.

I have a sense of timing. Though the bandages on my head were off two weeks ago and those in front of my eyes were to be removed last week, I insisted on delaying the procedure till yesterday, And today, with the cold-hearted precision of a diamond flashing its way through a sheet of glass, the light was let into my being. I am flooded by it. The nurse tells me that the voltage of the bulb in my room is very low, but, to me, looking at it is like staring at the sun. I cannot wait to really see the sun. It will flood my being. Surely I will be illuminated from within, when that happens... .

January 7

I am free today; great lightness of heart. Madness.

In anyone less level-headed than me, conditioned as I am by years of sober, moderate, middle class living, this king of euphoria could be dangerous. As it is, I caught myself making faces at the mirror. The last time I did that was when I was eight, before I lost my sight. How my face has changed! Not too bad for a man of 40 plus. Nice eyes, a bit deep-set; skin glowing with health, or is it happiness? Sensitive lips. And I like the touch of grey at my temples, rather distinguished, I think. Thanks to my fingers, I knew I had a well-formed face. But I did not know it looked so good. Madness. I'll be winking at the nurse next! There's so much to see. I want to visit distant lands, read all the books I couldn't read in Braille, see films instead of just hearing them. But the doctor says films, TV and bright lights are taboo for a while more... .

January 18

A strange thing happened tonight. It's 3 a.m. now. Other men, when they wake up at this time and are too disturbed to go back to sleep, will probably talk the dream over with the wife. Which brings me to something that cropped up at the office. At first I bristled when Mehta fawned on me and said a bit too loudly: "So, Sir, now you must find yourself a pretty wife, heh!" I laughed as loudly as the rest of them but my hackles were up, all the same. How crude can people get. Pretty wife indeed! And the thought seems to be doing the rounds... .

But I am digressing. I woke up because of a dream. It was so real that I am frightened. I was in a stinking hut, somewhere in a slum – there is this little girl playing outside the hut – and suddenly this man lurches out of the house. He totters drunkenly, eyes red-rimmed, heavy stubble on chin, arms held at odd angles from his skinny, ill-dressed frame, one hand clutching an empty bottle. An alcoholic. He stands blinking at the sunlight, weaving on his feet. He shakes the bottle and tilts it into his mouth... . Makes a face – it is empty. "Bai!" – he bellows drunkenly. He sees the little girl and blunders up to her. She shrinks back in utter fear. "Where's your mother?" he thunders. The girl stares up in dumb fright, mouth working, one pink ribbon fluttering crazily against her face.

The man yanks her up by her arms. And when she starts crying, he crashes one arm into the side of her head. "Tell me," he screams, his face close to her, and her eyes close in terror. Angered beyond reason, he drops the bottle and catches the child by the neck – his hands closing in, tighter, tighter.... .

I can't breathe, I choke, splutter, wake! Phew, what a dream. But my eyes won't open. In the pulsating dark before me, I can still see the man's hands around the child's neck, a face distorted in fear, pain gasping for air, eyes bulging – face turning red, turning red, then purple, then cold, then hot.... .

January 19

Spoke to my doctor about my dream. He did not laugh or cluck his tongue or suggest that I see a shrink. I must admit I expected him to do at least one of these things. But he listened carefully, hearing me out as I went slightly hysterical over the narration, and then suggested I occupy the mind with light entertainment – a walk, maybe a play, a farce or a light film.... .

January 20

I went to see *Inqualaab* today. Got tickets thanks to

my smart Malayali clerk Varghese. He seems to know how to get things done at a moment's notice.

I confess some excitement as I walked past the crowds that thronged outside the theatre and the feeling that crowded my mind as the lights dimmed was unique. Strangely, it reminded me of some vague day in my childhood. Perhaps I had sat in a theatre then, sandwiched between Appa and Amma, watching the screen, waiting for the picture to come on.

The movie began well enough. That Bachchan chap can really hold one's attention, I must say. And that Sridevi girl is certainly not what I thought girls in Madras looked like in my youth.

Somewhere after the interval, right there on the screen, my dream slum appeared. No! This can't be! I screamed silently.... Then the child came into view and the camera panned to the man emerging from the hut – and I knew. I watched horror-stricken. The same hut, the same child with one red ribbon and one pink ribbon in her hair, the same man, the same hands, horny, calloused, squeezing, squeezing.... The reel ground on inexorably. But I couldn't bear to watch. I closed my eyes with my hands, and felt the sweat clammy against them. But the scene went on inside my head – face, now red, now purple, now blue, gasping, gasping....

I got up and struggled out of the hall. Nobody else seemed horrified by the scene. In fact, some of the people in the audience were even laughing. As if it was a funny scene. I have come straight home. I think I walked the entire distance – and am so shaken I cannot think straight. How did my mind dream up a scene from a film I had never seen?

January 22

When Dr. V. dropped in, I was just sitting down for dinner. My first meal in two days. Munniamma had cooked up *puliodarai* and *vettals* to tempt me, though I do not normally eat rice at night. The doctor's coming was a welcome thing. He was quite informal and pulled up a chair and shared my meal. Perhaps it was an extension of his bedside manner – a tableside manner.

I finally gave in and explained, after much hedging, about the *Inqualaab* episode. He had seen the film – his wife is an avid film goer – and now for the shock! He says very positively that there is no such scene in the film.

Did I imagine it, I ask him? He shakes his head. But does not answer. I push my food away. Fear is uncurling in my stomach again, my hands grow numb; the chill spreads all over my body.

January 25

Dr. V. and a senior neuro-surgeon had a chat with me. It seems I have made medical history. A one-in-a-million case, though not enough operations of brain tissue transplants have been done to establish the statistics! Here's anyway what the learned doctors told me and only then I realised, what a serious operation I had undergone. An entire slice of brain from a donor was introduced in my brain. Obviously, the injury I sustained as a child had damaged that area of my brain which monitors information received by the eyes, which is why I could see hazy, lighted areas, but make nothing out of them despite my eyes being whole and intact. The transplant never ran the risk of rejection. That was one thing I needn't fear; the so-called blood-brain barrier was a natural biological fence that blocked the body's immune system from detecting the presence of foreign tissue and triggering off a rejection. In fact, he said, I was not even being given any rejection suppression drugs – they were not necessary.

The problem, in my case, lay elsewhere.... .

I have the mind of a woman mixed up somewhere in the labyrinth of neurons under my skull.... . The donor of this bit of feminine brain was one Shakubai of Koliwada. Thirty-one years old. Mother of three. Died in a municipal hospital of unknown causes. Ha! Ha! The joke's on me. I, a high-born Brahmin, descended from a long line of scholars and administrators, carrying the cells from an unclaimed corpse from the public mortuary... ! Talk about caste and the happy accident of high caste birth! Why? Let me tell you:

The police, after much poking around, discovered this, Shakubai had a tragic experience a few days before her death. Her drunken husband, in a fit of unreasonable anger, had strangled her young daughter to death with his bare hands. The experience had shattered Shakubai. The memory of the blows she had received at night bruised her mind, and she could not assimilate the horror of her own child being murdered before her eyes. She could only watch in stupefied desperation (the neighbours told Dr. V. later); not a movement, not a word, till the child's neck dangled brokenly from her husband's hands. Then, when it was too late, she came alive, screaming. Her eyes staring, mouth frothing, she threw herself aside with the violence of a flyswatter crushing a fly and tottered away.

"The story convinced us you were not affected mentally," Dr. V. said in his most reassuring manner. Before I could expostulate, they went on to explain by turns, what exactly they thought was the reason for my seeing the sequence so clearly. "Obviously, we must have touched a nerve that led to the subconscious, or the superconscious." Obviously, the transplanted tissue must have carried some memory cells, or some portion of the brain that holds traumatic images – and my brain just absorbed the waves of shocking experience witnessed by the brain that was grafted into mine. It all seems very impossible, I am not able to explain it in lay language very well, and I am not sure it is not a tale trumped up by the two doctors to jolt me into sanity. I have been left to mull over their little nugget of information for the time being. Small comfort, this!

February 1

Exactly, a month since I began to see. How dependent I have become on this, my borrowed slum women sight! Somehow, the verbal treatment seems to have worked. No more visions. But, I'd rather not speak too soon.

February 6

So help me God, that dream again.... As I sat reading a magazine in the office at lunch hour, and my eyes were open. One moment I was looking at the page, then it unfolded before me like a flag. The familiar slum, the child, the ribbon against its face, the face now blue, now purple....

I screamed in fear, and Varghese came running. Obviously, I had fainted, for Dr. V. was hovering over me when I recovered consciousness. He says he wants to have a long talk with me.

February 10

Varghese is a real boon. He has made over his evenings to me thrice a week. He says he wants me to teach him music. I teased him a little, asking him if he was planning to get married and he actually turned red. Funny, I have never seen anyone blush before. Actually blush. Anyway, he comes on Mondays, Wednesdays and Saturdays and I am rehearsing my *sa re ga ma pa* as if I am the novice. It is quite a pleasure teaching him, he has a resonant voice and is quick on the uptake.

February 11

Varghese is my main topic again. I have asked him to come four times a week, as I am dropping badminton on Fridays. Find it a bit too much. And music relaxes me more than running after a shuttlecock does.

Today when Varghese was singing, I noticed how the muscles of his neck stretched over the high notes. He has a knack of throwing his head up and singing from deep inside his throat. That makes for resonance, but the tendons of his neck really stand out and scream for attention. I found myself wondering how he would react if suddenly I put my hands around his neck to wring those chords.... I can imagine his expression had I asked him for his reaction. Now, thinking of it, I smile. But I really wonder how soft or hard his neck is to squeeze. If I curled my fingers around his voice box and pressed slowly – would he throw his head back further? Would the neck go taut? Or snap with a hollow crack? When he chokes, will his face turn red, purple-blue? I don't know how long I have been staring at this page but my hands are cold and trembling. I feel ill. Must wash my hands....

February 12

Am meeting Dr. V. today. Time I checked this strong

tendency for the sound of a neck snapping. A sickening thought. Is my personality being taken over by a few tissues from a dead woman's brain?

February 13

Dr. V. was quite alarming. At least in the process of calming me down, he got agitated, and he agitated me too. He says that my problem has to be tackled realistically. There is another way of beating it. He has consulted with a few other senior surgeons and they are hoping to carry out an experiment on me. Provided I am willing and let them do it.

The experiment is as follows: they will enter the back chamber of my eye – and give me a mild electric shock in the area that received the commands from the brain to the eye. It is all conjecture, Dr. V. warns me – there is no medical evidence that can help tell them where the exact spot is, which, when stimulated, or tired out, causes the hallucination. There is no way they know exactly which part of my brain sets the memory transplant from Shakubai's brain. So they will hunt around, and hope to hit the correct spot, among others.

February 20

Have given myself an ultimatum. I shall not think of the hallucination. Shall ignore the fact that my fingers curl around each other when I watch people talking; that I always watch people talking these days, not their faces, not their mouths and eyes, but their necks, their throats, the way the muscles move, sinuously, beckoning, beckoning....

I shall ignore the fact that the dream came upon me last night. And this time I woke up willing Shakubai to fall upon the darken brute of her husband, willing her to strangle the life out of him with the same careful deliberation that he had used on her child.

Resolution: I shall not think of the "should I, shan't I?" aspect of the operation either. Considering I am perfectly normal as long as I am not in the throes of the hallucination – and have the will power to keep myself from actually strangling somebody – I shall bide my time. Defer any decision. I have already rung up Dr. V. and told him to wait till mid-March. March 15, I shall tell finally whether I want to risk the operation or not.

March 1

The suspense is unbearable. Now I keep wondering why the dream has not recurred. Was it a passing phase? Post-operative trauma? Was Dr. V's diagnosis all wrong? Or is a new madness lurking in the wings, waiting to strike? Incidentally, I cut my hands today. Gripped my paper cutter when I tried to stop them reaching out to grasp the peon's throat – and did not notice how the blade cut into my flesh. Have bandaged it crudely – and cooked up a story about broken windows for tomorrow.

March 4

Phoned Dr. V. I am getting worse. Slowly, when the next hallucination comes, I know I will kill somebody. So, I've said yes for the operation. That's it. I won't think any more about it!

March 6

The date is March 8, Tomorrow, I enter the clinic. What a change from the last time in December. This time

I'm walking with my eyes open but my mind closed. Barred from within. But it's either this or bars in a mental asylum room I think. Maybe I will be a new man. Maybe I will go back to where hope picked me from. The dark ages. No, I am sure all will be well. ....

News item in a daily paper.

SURGEON DEAD

Bombay, March 8

In a freak accident, eminent eye surgeon Dr. Ved Prakash was strangled to death. The accident happened when a patient, while still under anaesthesia, suddenly seized the surgeon's neck and, before his hands could be disengaged, strangled the life out of him. Doctors on the spot said the patient was in the throes of some kind of hallucinating fit. Further details were not available.

3

NIGHT TRAIN TO GLASGOW

I DON'T KNOW when I nodded off into a light sleep, full of dark shadows chasing the landscape. The route from Birmingham to Edinburgh is long and, I realised, quite lonely. But locked inside my six-seater compartment, as the train rolled through the damp freezing autumn night, I felt surprisingly secure. I knew this was England and that the guard outside, knowing I was a lonely woman and a foreigner at that, would keep a watch on my compartment. I spent part of the evening talking into my recorder, dictating my observations at the Institute of Parapsychology in Birmingham. Then, the beauty of the cold, moon-drenched night outside the compartment captured my attention. I rested my head against the glass pane and, breathing deeply the beauty of the countryside, let my mind unravel. Somewhere along the route, sleep crept upon me and claimed me for its own.

It was perhaps the cold air that came in as she entered that released me from my haunted dreams. I woke up to see that the woman, seated on the berth opposite me, was ravishingly beautiful. She was like nothing – no one – I had ever seen before. Not in India and definitely not in England where the women, I felt, were pallid and dull. This woman was definitely different – her hair black and full of sparks, spilling like a fur coat over her shoulders and below, her brows a clear but rich gold, bronzed by the sun. She was dressed in somewhat unusual clothes for England too – confirming my fleeting idea that she was probably Scottish or Irish. Her dress was of some wild design in black and red, in a light netted material, as if the autumn air was of no import. It hung loose and full at the neck, to fall in folds over her breasts. By her side was a high large bassinet. A pink curtain made of the same netted material as her dress hung around its handle, protecting the contents within.

But it was her eyes which caught my attention and made me stare, losing all sense of courtesy. They were large and round and brown, most unusual in that part of the world, doubtless, but unusual eyes by any standard, of amazing depth and beauty. As she stared out of the window, lost in her thoughts, the light from the moon lit the luminous orbs of her eyes – turning the brown in them now gold, now almost a tawny red. I had never seen such beautiful eyes before.

She must have noticed my gaze lingering so unabashedly on her for she caught my eye in the reflection in the glass and smiled. She turned her head before I could move my eyes and looked me full in my face. I hid my confusion and murmured something about how beautiful the moon was.

She smiled again, then asked, "Are you a foreigner?"

Her voice was resonant and full, but I had an apprehension of cold, as of the night outside. Then the guttural quality of her words, the bark of her syllables, caught my attention. I answered.

"I'm from India," I said, "I'm visiting England,

working for my Ph.D. And you?" I asked, curiosity again getting the better of my normal reserve. "Are you from Scotland? Or…"

"India," she said, her eyes far away and golden in thought. "How beautiful the moon is on the Taj Mahal."

I could imagine the scene – how perfect her alabaster beauty would look beside the pulsating marble. I asked her whether she had been to Agra.

She shook her head, her hair bristling with the movement. "I never did," she said, "but I read. I see pictures. And I dream." She lapsed into another dream. Suddenly remembering my question, she said, "I am from Europe; I am also on a visit."

She turned to look at the bassinet tenderly, a fond look, then meeting my questioning gaze, smiled, "My babies."

"Twins?" I asked

She nodded. "A boy and girl. Very small," she said, laying one hand on the bassinet with a protective gesture. Her fingers were long, curved perfection, her nails a deep glowing red.

We got talking, I told her of my studies in parapsychology and how I was now off to Scotland, where I was told there were records in plenty, of things beyond the imagination that could feed my thesis on "The Impact of Surroundings on the Mind." I would break journey at Glasgow that night, stay for a day, then go to Edinburgh.

She showed surprising interest; surprising because her halting English had made me think she was slow of understanding. Now I realised that her mind was pointed and sharp and that it was only the language that had slowed her down.

NIGHT TRAIN TO GLASGOW

She asked me what I had discovered in the Midlands and I told her about the rather disappointing material I had gathered. I hoped for better stuff from Scotland, I said. I planned to go on to Ireland and round off my trip with a visit to the dark, forbidding area of Dartmoor, Thomas Hardy's country. Surely there I would find some proof of the power of matter over mind – in the dark surroundings.

"In Transylvania, where I come from, you will find many, many materials," she said and, for a moment, my hair almost stood on end along the length of my arm.

To my overwrought imagination fed by Bram Stoker and company, Transylvania meant ghouls – the Count Dracula and other such. I stared, to my embarrassment, and must have shown my shock for she threw back her head and laughed, the laughter running in ripples up and down her throat, her hair crackling, now amber, now black with the movement of her head.

"No," she said. "Transylvania today is a modern place – how do you say it – an urban society. We have no counts, and only a few castles remain – for the tourist to visit."

I said, "Of course," and bit back the questions that rose but she heard them nonetheless.

"But if you want, for your thesis, as you say," she said, "I can give you a fine story."

I nodded vehemently, and my hand moved stealthily to the recorder, to switch it on, unnoticed by her. I did not want to miss a word of her story and her accent often confused me.

"I can tell you so many stories," she said. "Transylvania is modern today. We have planes, buses and trains – though not like this, so nice – but the people, they are still haunted." She smiled at my look, then continued. "Haunted, I mean, by the past. It is too strong."

I did not understand and yet I did. "In India too, we are haunted by our past, our traditions won't let us be," I said. She seemed to see I understood. "But more," she said, "it is evil, the country, it will not let its people live in peace. It disturbs." I thought she meant bloodshed and warfare, but she said, "The horror you read is still true, the people still suffer for the sins of their forefathers."

"Look at me," she said, "so lonely, so doomed." Her eyes glittered, moist for a moment. Defiantly, she shed the mood and went on, "I am married to an American, rich and famous. I have everything. Everything a woman can want but my past haunts me. I live in torment. When the moon shines bright, my mind – how shall I say it – walks, paces – stalks the empty forests of my home in Virginia, USA. My husband cannot understand; he gets angry. 'Why are you so restless?' he asks. 'You are beautiful, why are you restless?' But beauty and money," she uttered a sound of contempt, "What can they do to stop the misery of my heart?"

"I left him," she said, her voice a moan of pain. I looked at the floor, embarrassed at this outpouring of emotion. "I left him to go where my heart leads, I wanted to go to Scotland, to walk the hills there. I told him, let me go, when I return I may not be restless any more, He agreed. He loves me very much. And before my children were born, I left him and came to England."

"You mean," I began. She cut me short. "He loves me. He could not see me suffer, so he let me come. I gave birth alone in the house I had rented. I knew my time was due and knew how to care for myself. Now I am ready to go to Scotland and listen to my heart speak."

I marvelled at her cool confidence in herself. I could

not imagine travelling in such a state as she described, let alone bearing children without the safety of a hospital and an entire medical staff at my service. But I was a weak, tradition-bound Indian (despite my defiant move outwards to tour England on my own) and she was probably, for all her beauty, tough, bred in the mountains, of peasant stock, of a hardy, no-nonsense race. I envied her.

"And now?" I asked. "What will you find in Scotland?" She shrugged her shoulders, which I suddenly realised were bare under her mantle of hair. The cold was like a caress to her, while even in the warmth of the compartment I could feel myself shivering off and on.

"I do not know," she replied. "But my heart says go and I go. Maybe I find peace. It is a wild country, so beautiful."

"I hear they have wolves and deer in the hills and that fogs and mists hang over the mountains through the year," I said.

She smiled. "Very beautiful," she said, "and more, I find peace there. I know." She talked on, hinting of a haunted life, growing up in a mountain place where wolves howled by day and hunted by night. "The cry of the wolf, it makes my blood stop in my veins. My great-grandfather they say was a wolf," she said.

I stared at her. She was mad. Beautiful and mad. Maybe I should call the guard, I thought, but curiosity held me where I sat transfixed. "A wolf!" I heard myself say, my voice considerably higher than usual.

She took my fear for interest. "Yes," she said, "You can put it in your book, your — what is it? — thesis. A wolf, a manwolf, like you say in English, a werewolf. That is why I am so restless. My past haunts me, as it does every person in my country. Now do you understand?" Her eyes held mine long and hard – mesmeric, raving.

The door opened, I almost died of fright but it was only the old guard. "Glasgow station, madam. You have five minutes."

I thanked him, and got up to get my things together. I switched off the tape recorder. I would have ample time to examine its contents tomorrow. Right now, I was happy to escape my strange but beautiful companion.

My movements disturbed the sleepers in the wicker bassinet, I heard a series of grunts and sniffs, like children waking from sleep. "They are awake, my babies. Hungry too!" she said.

"May I look?" I asked.

She smiled strangely, and curled back the curtains to let me peer.

My surprise made her laugh – a full throated laugh that fully indicated what a fool I had been made of. There, shuffling and snuffling, tail to nose, lay curled two of the furriest puppies I had ever seen. "Aren't they beautiful?" she asked, and I, confused, ashamed of my credulousness, nodded, looking away collecting my luggage. Silly Indian, she must be thinking. How easy to fool a superstitious oriental.

"I hope you enjoyed whatever high it gave you, fooling me like this," I said, my anger directed as much at myself as at her. "I suppose even the Transylvania bit was for effect." She smiled and my anger rose in proportion to the mockery in her smile. "I suppose you rich well-bred women get bored; You have the money, the beauty, and everything comes so easy to you that life gets boring. Then you invent situations, create nightmares that, once they're over, make your dull overplush lives seem worthwhile."

My words had their effect. She looked troubled. "I'm sorry – I thought…" she began. I cut her short. "You thought," I said, heaving my luggage out of the door, "You thought here's one way to make a boring journey interesting." The thought struck me – if those puppies hadn't woken – if I had not asked to see them, I would have left here believing the story was true. 'You're a terrific actress, though," I said as a parting short. "Why don't you ask your husband to let you join the movies?"

Before she could recover from that, I turned and left.

The guard smiled good night as I tipped him. He handed my bag down to me. It was then I realised that the recorder still lay on the berth, hidden in the bedclothes. There was barely time before the train moved. I rushed in and barged into the compartment.

She sat there, her eyes closed, her hand thrown back. Her blouse was unbuttoned at the neck and all the way down the front. Her hair covered her breasts. It took me a whole minute, as I stared wide-eyed, to realise that hidden in her hair, the colour of their fur matching it exactly, the two pups stood, paws moving in unison, as they sucked greedily.

She opened her eyes, gave me a look that was a million years old and smiled an inexplicably sweet smile. I picked up my recorder and fled into the safety of the night.

I left the tapes behind at Glasgow when I took a day train to Edinburgh two days later. The sound I heard on them, whenever I recall it, can still make my hair stand on end.

All they emitted was one lone, low fiendish night howl.

4
NIGHTWATCH

SHE WOKE UP at night to hear the wind howling. How it roared and shrieked... as if it were going to rush the little house into the valley below. She gritted her teeth and tried to go back to sleep, willed herself to go back to her dream... but the wind intruded.

When Sheila first came to Mussoorie, the wind had been there, of course. It had thrilled her then. After her long years in the plains, there was something romantic in the fact that the curtains were always billowing, the trees constantly whispering. Only in the harshness of the winter she had wished the wind would blow softer. The shrieking torrents that rushed through the cracks of their wooden house scared her on long, cold nights.

But these days, the wind shrieked all the time. There was some theory about deforestation being the cause of the increased fury, but all she knew was that it made a mess of her nerves.

She remembered now her evening battle with Mala, who had been quite unreasonable, really, but perhaps she had overreacted too. She always did, these days. But surely it was silly of Mohan agreeing to Mala's going to that picnic. After all, she should have been consulted. A moonlight picnic indeed, and Mala saying she had been to one before, without her knowledge, and would go again. And her friends – Sheila distrusted those friends Mala was so secretive about. She rose from her bed and walked the cold floor to Mala's room. The door was closed. She pushed gently and peered in. Mala sat on her bed, reading. The girl looked up, startled. The book fell from her hands. "Gosh Mummy, you scared me!"

"What are you doing? It's almost 2.30!"

"I woke up some time ago and couldn't go back to sleep. So I thought I'd do some reading," Mala said. There was a sullen note in her voice, but she was obviously minding her manners.

Mala looked at her where she stood. There was no welcome in her gaze, and Sheila felt an intruder there, in her daughter's room. The girl had circles under her eyes, she certainly needed her sleep. Perhaps she had been unduly rough on her. After all, the picnic was to take place within sight of the compound gates. "Mala," she said suddenly, "I think you can go to that picnic."

"Mum... my!" With a leap, Mala was across the bed, hugging her.

Tears filled Sheila's eyes, stupidly. Softy, she mocked herself as she hugged her daughter back. "You must not stay too long, and promise you will wear a coat."

The sun was streaming in through her window and the wind had died down when she woke again. She lay in bed, trying to remember if she had indeed spoken to Mala the night before.

"Wake up, sleepyhead," Mohan called from the next room. "Mala has prepared a lovely breakfast for you and you don't want it to get cold, do you?" So, she had spoken to Mala the night before.

As she hurried out of bed, Sheila felt apprehensive again. Mohan was going to Delhi tonight on one of his official trips and she wished she had not given her consent for the picnic. She hated to be alone. And yet she could not be sure what she dreaded more, being alone in the house, or being alone with Mala. The last time Mohan had gone out of town, she had a terrible row with the girl, over something she did not even remember now.... She checked her thoughts. This was no way to feel about your own daughter. "But where is the girl I loved?" she thought miserably.

Despite her forebodings, the day went pleasantly enough, as it always did when Mala was in good spirits. Only, that was not quite so often now, Sheila thought dryly to herself. Mala was cheerful only when having her own way; one little 'no' and the world collapsed around their heads. "Adolescence," Mohan said, every time she tried to put her foot down and contain Mala's tantrums. "Growing pains," he called them at other times, but Sheila knew he was being indulgent. She had also passed through adolescence and surely her mother had never had to face tantrums like the ones she weathered.

Mala was being quite mysterious that morning. She had gone to the Mall, shopping basket slung on one arm. "Getting some groceries for the picnic, Mom. Do you want some too?" she had yelled from downstairs while Sheila was packing Mohan's suitcase. Usually she made such a fuss to go shopping with her. "I hate those messy stores, they are so crowded," she'd protest and Sheila would have to drag her along.

"Just get me a loaf of bread for Daddy's sandwiches,"

she had called back, thinking – when it's her picnic – then stopped herself short again. This would not do, she was turning into a nag.

By evening, the cold had set in again. She closed the windows and felt herself getting tense as she battled with the latches against the rising force of the wind. The happy mood of the day was gone with the sunshine. The long night would tick slowly by, she thought, watching with an increasing dread the sunset beyond the mountains. The clouds formed mock peaks against the sky, closing in on all available space. The place was getting on her nerves, she ought to take a holiday.

The moon rose slowly that night, flooding the slopes with a silver light and even her nameless tension could not dispel the haunting beauty.

"A perfect night for a picnic," she said across the dining table to Mala. Mala nodded, eyes bright with excitement. "The circles under her eyes are darker tonight," Sheila thought, "and tomorrow they will be darker." Dinner was a fiasco, with Mala too excited to eat and Sheila thinking of the loneliness ahead.

They came when Mala was in her room, putting her coat on. At first Sheila thought it was a branch knocking against the roof, but when the sound persisted, she opened the door.

The cold rushed in, filling the house with its presence. A group of girls stood outside. huddled together. "Is Mala ready?" one of them asked.

"Come in," she said, opening the door wider. But the girls only shuffled their feet and continued to huddle across the doorway. "No, thank you, Aunty, we are loaded."

Her eyes focused on a shape on the floor and she

discerned a large gunny bag at their feet. "What a lot of stuff for a small picnic," she said, laughing. "What's in it?"

The girls looked at each other – then at the bag. As if she had asked them to reveal state secrets, she thought.

"Eats," said one. "A *dari* to sit on, and extra blankets," another added. At least they won't be cold, Sheila thought.

"Ready," Mala announced, coming down from her room, her black plastic bag heavy on one arm. Her right hand was bandaged at the wrist. "Oh, the can opener slipped when I was trying it out," she volunteered, seeing Sheila's eyes on her wrist.

"Did it bleed much?" Sheila asked, then seeing her daughter's eyes cloud over with irritation, she changed the topic. "More eats?" she asked lightly, looking at the black bag, and one of the girls tittered in the dark.

"Bye, Mummy, I'm off..." and they were gone into the night before she could say all she had wanted to say about their being back soon, about taking care to keep warm...

She could see them from her bedroom window, she realised with a start. She had been making a fuss, really. Just a girlish get-together, Enid Blyton style. After all, other mothers had said yes to the picnic. Only... had the boys been waiting elsewhere, while the girls collected Mala?

She went to bed, refusing to worry, refusing to hear the whisper that screamed fear inside her head each time she was alone in the house....

And awoke with a start. The house was quiet. What had woken her up? Mala, she should be back. The clock showed 10.30 in the luminous dial. She moved to the window.

The shapes were there. Sitting in a ring. They had managed to get a small fire going – she could see them in the firelight, sitting shoulder to shoulder, huddled in woollens. They seemed to be clapping and swaying. The familiar rhythm eluded her for a moment, then she got it – it was one of those names-of-things games – where you changed names to the beat of handclaps. Girlish games never changed, she thought with a smile as she went back to bed again.

As she lay in bed, holding her mind steady for sleep, she could hear the chanting almost. Be quick – then high-pitched laughter as a voice faltered….. then a murmured consultation, Then the voices started again. Foul and fair, be quick, rotten air, be quick, fair and foul…. rising in speed and pitch…till the shrillness woke her, and only the wind howled outside.

Eleven o'clock, the timepiece said – she had dropped off for twenty minutes and dreamt all the voices! She leapt out of the window. The fire burned brighter now and the girls were still sitting around it. They were eating, she saw them reaching out and picking things from the baskets in the centre. They should be home soon enough, she thought. Once the food is over, the fun is done. "Finish the food, and the mood," she remembered. She tried to spot Mala in the circle, to see if she was eating, but the shapes were too indistinct, wrapped in their shawls and blankets, to be recognisable.

What a night, she thought—till this child returns, I can't get any sleep. She caught sight of her face in the dressing table mirror. How pale she looked and how lined her skin had become… those lines on either side of her mouth made it look so drawn. She smiled – lifting the mouth in a curve – and her face transformed itself into youth. Why, Mala looks like me, she thought – noticing the resemblance for the first time. The idea gave her pleasure and, still smiling, she lay in bed again.

And slept. To dream of cries at night, strange knocking and maniacal winds that toppled trees, picked them up again to lightly carry them across the meadows and hurl them into the valley below... while shapes rose and fell, rose and fell and changed around the fire...

Mala — she came awake once more. Surely it was Mala knocking. She rushed to the window, but the shapes were still there around a fire that had almost burnt out. And they were dancing. Not Western style, but with strange, jerky movements, round and round the fire. Something nagged her memory — she had seen such a dance somewhere... But she couldn't remember. At a school function? A Shakespeare play? A film? She let it be, watching the dancers. The clock stuck 12.30. She ought to go down and fetch Mala, she thought. Mohan would be angry that she had allowed her out so late after midnight.

But the thought of the cold outside kept Sheila standing where she was. And she could not be a spoilsport. She watched the dancers again. Round and round, up and down, round again... she realised with a start they were moving further away. The fire was outside the circle now — between the dancers and the house.

The girls were moving towards the edge of the meadow, not knowing they did so in their preoccupation with the rhythm. Again the dance movements nagged her memory, then panic took hold. The girls would fall off... the wind would blow them over...

She could almost see one of them toppling over and disappearing into the void, and she could see the shocked reaction on the other dancers' faces...

She throttled a scream at the image, grabbed a

blanket from her bed and rushed out of the house, the wind roaring behind her.

The long run into the night sobered her a little – and she arrived panting but sane, to the edge of the area lighted by the fire. The girls were still dancing, holding sticks in one hand, jerking their bodies up and down. No wonder they felt no cold, she thought.

The circle broke, the dancers quietened. And formed a line. They stood with their backs to her, now clutching their sticks in front of them. She could hear a slow chant begin – try, try, try... the words said. Some girl guide song, she thought, the tune so eerie. It rose and fell like the wind, the voices rushing over the words.

The girls started moving forward, one step at a time, still chanting their song. Try, try, try... and as they rushed forward in one gasp, the wind howled and pushed and she heard the words clearly this time.. fly.. fly... and the brooms on the sticks.

Sheila screamed in the dark – hurrying the bodies to the edge of darkness; hell-bent on madness, over the brink.....

5

EXCHANGE COUNTER

THE CLERK LOOKED at him for a while. Hugo thought there was a strangeness about the look. For a fleeting moment, he had the impression that the man had recognised him. But that was impossible. The flicker in those dull eyes as they focused on him, after the clerk had stared his full at the gay green and red fibre glass chairs of the airport lounge, was possibly the man's only way of showing interest. There was no doubt about his being quite unknown.

The clerk bent his cadaverous face quite close. Too close. The smell of his breath hit Hugo like a punch in the face. "You want how much change?" he hissed, his eyes holding Hugo's mesmerically.

Hugo panicked. There had been some mistake. He had heard wrong. No, this was preposterous. He wasn't there to change money, he was there for another kind of change. But suddenly...

"How much change?" the clerk rasped, almost knocking him out with his fetid breath. And the eyes flickered knowingly again.

Hugo felt his palms grow moist. His upper lip beaded

EXCHANGE COUNTER

with anxiety. But he went on – bold in his desire to end the suspense. "A woman – my wife, she needs change," he said, wondering at his own audacity. He had, he realised, chosen his words well. They hung there, almost visible, waiting to be absorbed. If only the clerk would close his mouth!

The clerk made a quick motion with his head. A half jerk. A smile that was more like a nervous grimace. But Hugo relaxed. He was not going to be handed over to the police, after all.

"Come in, you step here," – the clerk motioned to the floor with his hand. Looking down, Hugo found a small hook holding the front of the exchange counter to the wall. He unlatched it, and it swung open. With one swift look backward into the crowded airport lounge, he stepped in.

The clerk motioned him to a stool. The area was bigger than he thought – the space behind it extended into near darkness. Lucky there's so much space, Hugo thought – he didn't quite fancy being closely confined with the clerk's breath. Pulling his stool as far back as possible, he seated himself. Waiting. Today at last, he would be able to do something he'd always hoped for, dreamed about, prayed for. Never expecting it to happen, of course – but sometimes obviously, hopes were answered, and prayers listened to! If all went well, Hugo would be a free man again. When he went home, he would not be entering his prison – but a new freedom. For, with Julia, the jailer, gone, the prison would disappear too. Freedom. Hugo breathed in deeply, and looked up to the counter, and beyond it into the lounge.

It wasn't there! There was no lounge with people flocking to the fibre glass chairs. No loudspeakers purring arrival and departure schedules in indistinct confusion.

Nothing, nothing at all.

He held his breath—the clerk had spoken; was speaking still. "They are all there—only you can't see them. They can't see us either, we are in another dimension," he said smiling. Hugo was reminded of the dentist's smile just before he clamped the pliers around his rotten tooth, and he winced. But the surprise still held him numb. Too numbed for fear.

"Only those who know of the exchange counter can see it," the clerk explained. "I know how you feel, but you'll get used to it," he added reassuringly. Hugo smiled somewhat wanly.

That explained it. Explained why, when he had seen the abandoned exchange counter at the Santa Cruz airport the first time, it had looked so dilapidated and deserted. Just a shack-like shell with no one behind the counter. No lights. Only the words: Exchange: Cambio: Currency painted on the top. "When the international airport came up, they shifted them and the machinery there — and left this for us," the clerk said, almost reading his thoughts. "If you had not heard about us, you'd never have been able to see me."

Hugo thanked the day he had decided to be a good husband and wait for Julia's two-hour late flight. Normally he'd never have come, but he had a day off — and the air-conditioned lounge was not a bad place to kill time in. He had almost fallen asleep when he heard the voices talking near his shoulder. The men were sitting, backs to his back, and were oblivious to his presence. He discovered after a while that one was talking about how he had got rid of his mother-in-law. At the exchange counter. And it had worked! He had jerked awake with a start, startling the men, breaking the low hum of their voices. They had hastily

EXCHANGE COUNTER

walked away, even before he could see them. But in that minute Hugo's mind was made up. He'd 'exchange' Julia.

For the next few days, he had been full of doubts. Suppose the exchange counter men threw him out? Suppose it had been a carefully planned practical joke, planned on a sleeping man by a couple of pranksters? Suppose…. But he made bold.

And today. Today… "What is your wife's age?" The clerk spoke again. "Thirty-eight," Hugo said, coming back with a start. It was all impossibly true. The clerk was seriously filling a form, writing down details. "First name," he said, "Julia," Hugo replied. "Why do you want her exchanged?" the clerk asked. Hugo wanted to go into a barrage of replies – how he couldn't take her nagging any more, how her bossiness belittled him, how he writhed under the agony of the fact that she had a bigger salary and a more responsible job then he did – he was a sales representative to her executive status! But before he could begin, the clerk shook his head understandingly. "I understand," he said, and wrote furiously on the form. Hugo glanced in, the words made no sense – he realised with a start that they were in English, but unreadable. The clerk was writing backwards. Quite confidently, forming his letters with careless speed.

Hugo looked up to see the strange look on the clerk's face again. Recognition? Approval? What was it? But the man was talking once again. "It is necessary for your wife to come in person. You must come with her too," he said. "Only then can the exchange be effected."

"When can that be?" Hugo asked. Suddenly he couldn't wait. "Any time," the clerk said.

Hugo felt the elation swelling his veins.

"No time like the present," he murmured.

'My wife is arriving tonight — in fact, I have come to receive her," he said. "Can I bring her now?"

The clerk laughed, his laughter more foul breathed than his speech. "You are in a hurry, aren't you, sir?" he crackled. "Anyway," he added, "better to be quick. When both partners want an exchange, the first applicant is satisfied, rather than the second," he added.

Spoken like a true clerk, thought Hugo, who had a healthy hatred for clerks. But he refrained from saying anything. "Will today do?" he asked again. He looked at his watch. The face was blank. No numbers; no hands. "There is no time in this dimension," the clerk said, noting his gesture. "But anyway, go now and come back with her, I am waiting." A thought struck Hugo. "What will I have to pay? How much...?" Dash it, he did not even have too much cash on him. "Nothing," the clerk said, "You are giving us a gift of a soul, aren't you? All exchange subjects are irrevocably ours. That's enough," and he released the lock that let Hugo out into the teeming airport lounge again.

Julia looked as radiant as ever. How he hated her. And how quickly her radiance evaporated when she saw him. "Oh hell, I didn't expect you," she said. He felt the cold in her voice touch him like a hand, but refused to let his own coldness come through. The thought of the clerk waiting injected warmth into his voice. "Darling, I just thought I'd surprise you," he said. "Do you have any luggage?" Of course she did. Julia never travelled without her executive bag and her vanity case besides her office bag. So there was an hour or more to wait.

Hugo smiled and almost oiled the words across. "While we are waiting, can you do me a favour?" he asked.

EXCHANGE COUNTER

Julia looked at him, puzzled. They had stopped asking each other for favours a long while ago. "I have some money to exchange... someone gave me a few dollar bills... but only passengers can exchange currency... so will you...?" His words sounded lame to his own ears, but Julia followed him. She's not really puzzled, he thought. For once, she's not asking too many questions.

"Here, please," the clerk smiled. And before Hugo could hold his breath to avoid the stench, which had surely got worse since he had been here last, rough hands gripped his shoulders, he felt a stab, as of a hard knee against his backbone, and there was a whirring in his ears – like a pair of scissors going chop, chop, chop. He opened his mouth to scream, to say that there had been some mistake – the woman was the exchange subject... but the clerk's smile stopped him. "Sorry sir, but the first applicant gets the preference..." and the chop, chop grew louder and louder and engulfed his being. The last thing he saw was Julia, her hair swinging loose on her perfect back, walking triumphantly away – out of the counter into the space where he knew the well-lit lounge was!

6
I SPY

I HATE PARTIES. All my friends love them. Which is why, despite the fact that all the noise and high laughter makes me want to crawl into the wall, I attend them. New Year parties are the worst kind, somehow. The noise is louder, and the music even more jarring than at other times.

I had cornered a packet of chips — one of the few compensations parties offer — and made myself comfortable on one of the roomiest sofas in the place. Of course, I had taken the precaution of rearranging my face to look its scowliest best. When one has thick eyebrows and a beak of a nose like mine, it is not at all difficult to keep people at bay. I was eminently successful this time too.

I looked around the room, munching steadily. Quite a pretty room actually — if you could ignore the clutter. The furniture was wooden; old teak with a gentle fretwork pattern that repeated itself on the backs of chairs, the legs of the coffee table and the edges of the sofa set. There were pretty prints on the walls, or perhaps, knowing Winston, they were originals. I specially liked the one with horses snorting into a sea of frothing waves. The white manes flecked with foam reflected in the whites of their eyes and their arched necks held a tautness that created a tension in my back as I studied them.

The best thing about the room was the fireplace. White and brown wood, with an artificial fire. There was no need for a fire screen to hide this fireplace, and there was none. Any remnant of soot or black that might have layered the area in the years when logs and coal had sent sparks up the chimney, had been scrubbed scrupulously out. Winston's mother was nothing if not house-proud. Winston's many warnings about the carpeting and upholstery had made that obvious.

The room was getting warmer. It was a moonless night, quite, quite cold and the thick forest of pines that edged the holiday cottage made the wind howl. The windows had been closed quickly, when the first gusts of night air had blown in. The dancing had reached a pitch. I could see Sush doing the mad woman scene, flinging her arms overhead and jerking her head hard enough to get her whiplash injury – but it only meant she was enjoying herself. Little wonder too; she was dancing with Mohan. The others were having the lemonade laced with tiny dollops of gin – most of the gang was on the floor.

The music stopped suddenly – just when I was biting rather noisily into a bunch of chips. My ears sang with silence. Blessed silence. The collective groan that rose from the group on the floor at being stopped at mid-movement dissolved into silence too. Evidently no one else thought silence quite desirable. Everyone cluttered around the sound system – then there were cries of dismay.

"Hi there." I looked up at the voice. It was Mohan, standing looking down at me from his six feet plus. "Why are you so quiet today?" he asked. I smiled a watery smile and offered him the chips as a reply. It was not easy to talk when Mohan was looking at me. But Mohan did not seem to know that. He folded himself into the sofa and prepared to make earnest conversation.

He could be charming when he wanted and though I had outgrown my crush on him, I found myself blinking at him, and stumbling over my words – all the terrible teenage things I thought I had grown out of when I turned 21 last year.

We chatted about this and that and I realised I was enjoying myself. I even forgot to munch on the chips till Mohan reached into my lap for a helping. I looked up to see Sush standing nearby – glowering at me.

"Let's play a game – let's play 'I Spy'" – Sush looked away from me quickly and said in her loud, infectiously gay voice. The inertia that had settled upon the group lifted, moved and transformed itself into enthusiasm. "Yes, let's play something;" "who'll be it?" – the voices tossed about in the room; the merriment spreading like a virus.

I tried to disappear into the sofa. If there is one thing I hate more than dancing – it's games. And 'I Spy' heads my list of hatefuls! For one, I can sit out the dance but no one can be spoil-sport enough not to join in a game!

The last time we played 'I Spy,' Winston was a terror when it came to practical jokes; he had crept up on me as I hid behind a door and hooked a plastic bird claw into my neck, chuckling loudly. If I had an ECG soon after, they might have put me in intensive care – but, as it happened, I recovered, though slowly –and Winston moved to fresh terrors.

'I Spy,' it was again. And there was nothing to it. I hated Sush then for that moment, for her idea. Surely she could have found a better way of removing Mohan from my vicinity! And anyway – anyone could see Beetle Brows was no competition for Sush – so confident, so fair and pretty!

"Let's dim the lights!" Winston had torn himself away from the tape deck, and jumped into the spirit of the game. All his instincts for fun were jangling loud and clear. I sensed trouble. I was his favourite victim. He knew it too – for he announced "I'm the host, so I'll be It!"

The others cheered and applauded him – but I was ready to puke. He'd probably throw a spider at me this time, instead of saying 'I Spy.' And spiders were guaranteed ICU material!

The lights went out – I heard a high-pitched, very silly scream. It stopped the moment I realised my mouth was open and the sound was from my throat. "Relax," someone said, and Winston switched on a tiny blue light behind a picture to enliven the gloom. "Now hide!" – he ordered, and, in the darkness, his excited voice took on a new, unknown menace.

There was a hustle and a flurry as soon as Winston left the room. People bumped around into furniture, against each other; I heard Sush scream and then call out to Mohan in a stage whisper. She loved lights out – it meant smooching time.

I had to hide – and quickly. I thought briefly of walking out of the house – hiding outside till everyone else was found and then giving myself up. But the dark deterred me, and even toy spiders are preferable to live creepy crawlies. The wind was seriously setting down to an all-night howl and that was even more terrifying.

Cursing myself for being such a damp squib, and swearing to stay home with a fever next time, I scanned the room mentally for a hiding place.

I had it. The fireplace. There was room enough behind the artificial fire – the chimney had not been closed down nor the fireplace itself narrowed.

There was ample room for me to stand flat against the inside wall of the chimney. And no fear of spiders either, real or plastic. The place, I had noticed earlier, was sparkling clean, and besides, Winston would never, never dream I'd hide there. I crept around the darkness, dreading each moment – but, finally, my hands touched the cool red tiles of the fireplace. I stepped gingerly across the wide expanse of artificial coals, almost tripped over a wire – but made it to safety. Now, all I had to do was stand very, very still.

I hated the pinpricks of sweat the fear and excitement had caused; besides, the chimney smelt dank. I prayed fervently there were no bats hiding around – the mere thought almost sent me scuttling out. But I could hear Winston prowling about and periodic screams and grunts and an occasional deep-throated laugh told me the victims were being properly terrified. I opted for the bats.

I stood there for what seemed hours, but were actually minutes. In the dim light of the room, I could make out only dusky shapes. It struck me suddenly that this is how the monks of old must have felt – hidden away behind a chimney, or in a cubby hole while the inquisitors searched to take them to the rack. What happened if a family forgot about someone and left him to rot? The thought gave me goose pimples – this was not the time to think of such things – I was in a pretty tight corner myself. Stuck halfway up a chimney behind a fireplace that needed only the flick of a switch to be persuaded to impersonate Dante's Inferno!

With a start, I realised how quiet things were. Everyone had left the house. I bent to peer into the dark, and saw two shadowy forms against the wall.

"Gentle there..." – that was Sush's stage whisper. I froze. That was Mohan with her, I was sure, and it would not do to let them know I was near. I blessed the dark for its cloak of secrecy – it saved me the embarrassment of seeing them smooch, and it spared me from Sush. She'd fly into one of her infernal rages if she thought I was trying to spoil her fun.

"Let's go," Mohan said, to which Sush answered with a giggle. "Coward!," she, taunted, then more gently, "no one will come here, Winston's gone to look for Dipti in the woods. I told him she was hiding there and the others are in the hall." "How did you know?" Mohan asked. His voice sounded velvety in the dark. I imagined him talking in that voice to me in another time, another place – in another world – and I felt a quick rush of helpless emotion. "I don't know! I just sent him there, silly," Sush said. Then there were sounds of other voices as others entered the room. "But where's Dipti?" I heard Winston ask. "Outside," Sush replied, airily. "She'll freeze there, the wind is turning vicious," Mohan said – and I warmed to the concern in his voice. It almost made me crawl out – but I could imagine Sush's face when she found out I had been around, listening all the time! So I kept very still.

"Let's go and look for her, gang," Mohan said, and though I could hear Rani and a few others complain about the cold, the voices moved towards the door.

"I say, Winston," that was Sush again, her voice molten velvet, "can't we do something to feel warmer – can't we?" Then the hesitation went out of her voice, and enthusiasm replaced it, "Let's return to a warm welcome, what say you?" There was a pause which made me somewhat uneasy. Then I wondered what she meant.

What was she up to next? "What say you, Dipti?," Sush hissed, hidden from my view, but her voice so close, I could almost touch it. I understood then. Sush had known my hiding place all along; Sush was out to get me, after all. "Sure!" said Winston gallantly – and I heard the flick of a switch and the banging of the front door as they swept out into the windy night.

Inside, at my feet, the fire crackled and glowed and the ruby heat reached into the chimney, seeking the sky.

I could hear their voices, outside, faintly in the wind. They were calling out to me to come in to safety.

7

THE OLD MAN AND THE TREE

THE OLD MAN looked at the tree. It seemed to him that the tree had begun to understand him quite clearly now. There was a definite understanding in the twinkle the glossy leaves had as they moved before his gaze... and there was not even much of a breeze to move them, just then. "Don't worry," he murmured, "we'll find a way out, you and me. I won't let them cut you down."

He had planted the tree quite casually 35 years ago, when his daughter had turned six. It had been his special gift to her, something he felt would give her delight that would last through the year, even after the pleasure over her new clothes and the dolls had died down. The tree had survived, a hardy little plant, it had somehow thrived despite the predatory goats that wandered into the compound and despite the children's efforts to include it in their play. No one really took much notice of it except in the early summer, when touched by the warmth it suddenly responded by bursting into countless lacy flowers that feel like soft stars to carpet the ground in front of the house. His daughter and her friends would then spend whole evenings collecting the fallen blossoms into their frocks, and stringing clumsy garlands out of them.

But in the past years, after his wife's death and with his daughter far away, keeping house in a foreign land, the old man had begun to notice the tree again. Somehow he felt happier sitting outside, under its shade, reading while the light played hide and seek between the leaves. On winter afternoons, he even stretched out in his easy chair and had a quiet nap, imagining he heard the voices of his wife and daughter in the background. He always woke refreshed from such naps, shivering a little as the nip in the early evening air caught him unawares, but in his mind, there would be a warmth that made the long night bearable.

He would not admit it even to himself, but he felt his daughter had left behind a little of herself with the tree. And they wanted to cut it down. How could he allow it to happen?

Not that he could see any way of preventing it, though. The old man sighed as he remembered his last chat with his son about the tree. Dinesh was a good boy, not as responsive to his heart as Radha his daughter had been, but in all ways a dutiful son. No one could deny that. But there was a stubborn streak in him, his mouth could curl downward in just that way his wife's had done, and that was the end of that argument. He had never been able to get past his wife's stubbornness, and Dinesh had the same easy victories.

He had broached the subject quite easily, ignoring the flutter in his heart. "Pass the *dal,* please," he had said, then "is it absolutely necessary to cut down that tree?" "Yes," Dinesh's answer had confirmed his fear. He was going to make an issue of it. "I have told the landlord that he can go ahead and cut the tree, if it interferes with his plans," Dinesh had continued, "so please don't make an issue of it, Father." The tables had been turned. So, now it was he who was making an issue out of it!

The landlord really did not need to cut the tree. The old man knew it. The new flats were coming up uncomfortably close to the old house but there was ample space to build the dividing wall without disturbing the tree. It was just one of those thoughtless things the new generation was constantly doing, cutting this, removing that, in its acquisitiveness; till the last pillars of society would crumble. There was no point in explaining this to Dinesh though, he was one of the same generation. He would think nothing of cutting a tree to build a flat...

He became aware that someone was calling, he turned around to see two khaki clad men standing outside the fencing. "We have come to cut the tree," one of them said, and his heart lurched nastily in despair. But he steadied himself, they did not look like tree cutters. Even as his mind raced ahead seeking excuses to delay the deed... the man explained that they were going to trim some of the branches since they interfered with the phone lines. He watched as the man scrambled up, and hacked away at the magnificent branches. The wail which arose, he felt, would surely pierce his eardrum... how surprising the men could not hear it. The branch lay bleeding across the compound the whole night, and he could hardly sleep for worrying about his daughter. The morning bought a glimmer of hope. Why would they trim a tree that was going to be cut anyway? Perhaps Dinesh had spoken to the landlord.

But Dinesh had not. It was just one of those things the telephone department did once in a while, trimming trees, and all that. Well, if Dinesh would not do anything about it, he would. He would approach the greater authority. He

THE OLD MAN AND THE TREE

did not speak to anyone of his decision. But that afternoon, he dressed almost furtively, stitching a hasty button on his white shirt, brushing out the fluff from the old trousers. His arms felt strangely exposed, and he decided that he would ask Dinesh to make him a long-sleeved shirt for Diwali. He tucked in a ten rupee note for what he told himself wryly was "official purposes," and hailed a rickshaw for the Corporation office.

The official whom he met was not interested. Yes, there was some campaign on the planting of more trees, specially in the forests, and trees, as the leaders of the country, had so rightly pointed out, were very necessary for preserving the rainfall quota and all that, but he was not sure that he could do anything to prevent a tree inside the town from being cut down. The old man would not give up, though. He passed on the ten rupee note. In his days, money had always made officials change their mind, and however much life was different now, he knew this could not have changed. The official pocketed the note without even looking at it and called for some paper, and noted his complaint in painfully written vernacular. The old man would have preferred Hindi, but the official said that his subordinates would understand the local language better. Yes, he would send somebody to investigate.

The old man reached home without a feeling of having achieved anything. Still the official had accepted the money, so there was hope.

He changed into his comfortable kurta again, and settled down under the tree, exhausted. The swishing of the leaves soothed his nerves, and he slipped into the familiar world of voices again.

He awoke with a start. Dinesh stood near his shoulder saying something. The tree men had come! He sat up hastily, stretching his eyes wide trying to keep awake completely. The girl who stood behind Dinesh smiled shyly. She was dressed in a 'salwar kameez,' and had a lot of bangles on...

"Father, this is Lata; with your blessings, she will be your *bahu*," Dinesh was saying. He rose quickly, saying, "Let us go inside, children, we can talk better there..."

But the girl stopped him. "Let us sit here," she said, her voice very soft and musical, "it is so pretty under this tree, like an enchanted place."

The old man smiled. He had a vision of priests, and prayers, of festivities and happiness. And the house would not be silent any more. Somehow, he knew, too, that his tree was safe now. He and Lata would see to that. He looked up at the leaves and, yes they had understood it too.

8

A BICYCLE FOR TWO

I CANNOT BELIEVE it – I am face to face with the greatest moment of my life. Freedom, adventure, escape – happiness, everything is suddenly within reach – practically in my grasp.

But let me begin at the beginning. Let me begin by telling you how this momentous change has occurred in my life. It's all thanks to Kaka, Ramukaka. A most unexpected source. He's not really my Kaka. I don't think he's anybody's Kaka.

Kaka – at least no one claims him as kith or kin. He's a somewhat sloppy old man, not completely sane – who lives with us. But he is kind to me – which Uncle Vinod isn't, and even dotes on me in his senile, stupid way.

I tolerate him. Sometimes, when Uncle Vinod's curses get too much to bear, it is good to have Kaka for an ally.

I really don't know what Uncle Vinod has against me – he's always picking on me, cursing, raging, especially when he's had a tough day at work and one drink too many, trying to relax.

Uncle Vinod can be vicious – I still wear the scar

he gave me when, in one of his infernal rages, he threw his glass at my head, four years ago. But I know no other parent and Uncle Vinod is father, mother and foe to me.

I tolerate him, because Uncle Vinod is a genius. He's taught me much I know — and when he lets me help him with one of his inventions, I feel a kinship with greatness.

You must have heard of Uncle Vinod — his name is in the news ever so often. Vinod Khurana. He has invented just about anything — from 3D video cassettes to automatic broomsticks. And often I've helped and watched, and taken notes for him. And one day I know he'll let me work on his very secret invention. I don't know what it is — he keeps it locked in an underground room. But for how long? One day I'll be allowed in.

That is why I put up with Uncle Vinod. Though it hurts to be hated. And screamed at. And hit.

See how the rancour pours out. See how the wound to my ego festers and bursts open! Yet I soothe myself with the balm of forgetfulness. I do not have an option. So I live without hate. And without love. With Uncle Vinod.

But I digress. I'm not writing this to record my relationship with this man. This is to be a diary where I will record all the fantastic events that will follow this day.

But let me start again — at the proper beginning. Yesterday, on February 29, 1992, Kaka came to my room at night. It had been a bad day, and a worse evening.

Uncle Vinod had got snarled again, unable to unravel one of his very secret problems. And he found some papers missing. Of course he suspected me — though I had not been in the house all day.

So all hell had broken loose — he might have killed me, if I had not escaped to my room as the drink began to overpower him.

I was sitting on the bed, cursing the day I was born. Cursing myself, for not having the guts to break free of the relative comforts of a loveless home – when Kaka came in. Quietly, like a partner. I looked up in surprise – his agility was unusual. He came up to me, and put his hand on my hair – a gesture he frequently performs – and which never fails to irritate me. I hate his slobbering familiarity as much as I hate uncle's wild rages. But just then, I sat without moving away. Even Kaka's slobbering love seemed better than the mood of self-hate I had fallen into.

Kaka drew out a roll of papers. And then sat down before me. I looked through them – wondering what he was up to – it took me one look to realise they were uncle's missing papers.

Surprise – anger, how can I explain the plethora of emotions that took hold of me. I had suffered uncle's rages all day, in spite of being innocent; and here this bumbling fool was placing the papers he had stolen before me as if it was some prize offering.

I rose in my chair – ready to shake him by the hair. But the look in his eyes stopped me.

"Baba!" he said, he always calls me Baba, for some unknown reason. "Don't be angry with an old man like me. I am old enough to be your father and you have always been like a son to me." Son, I thought, my foot. But his words blocked my thoughts again.

"These drawings are the end of a long search," he said. "I have waited and watched and waited years for them.

"You do not know my story," he continued "and this is not the time to tell it. I will not say more than this – that I am a being lost, lonely, damned. Damned by my own knowledge, doomed as much by my lack of it.

"I live in a vacuum, and would have given up my life long ago, except for the one hope that kept me alive.

"This" – he pointed dramatically at the role of papers lying on my table – "how I have waited and watched for this."

'And now," he continued, while I sat, feeling more and more as if I was listening to some strange tale of fantasy – feeling more and more certain the old man was mad – "now, you are my only chance. With these papers, you can help restore me to life."

He reached out and took the papers in his grasp, and curved his other hand around my arm. "Come with me – I'll show you something I've never shown anyone else before," he said.

I followed – disbelieving, but yet entranced. The man was mad – but I was inclined to humour him. For now at least we walked the dew-drenched lawns till he reached the edge of the compound to his own little shack. I had never entered it in all the years he had lived there – and the mess he lived in only vindicated the fact. He led me still deeper, through the first room, a tiny place where he obviously cooked and ate and slept, to a large inner room.

The room was bare, except for an old cycle that stood in a corner – an old cycle, I say, because such bikes had gone out of style even before I had graduated from tricycles – but for all other purposes, this could have been a newly crafted one. It shone dully in the light of the 20 watt bulb that shone in the room; and there was not a sign of rust on its gleaming metal. I stared – first at Kaka, who stood staring at the bike as if at his first sight of godhood, and then at the antique. There was nothing unusual about the bicycle, except for a fancy contraption that was stuck on to the handlebar, and from which wires ran to the pedals. "This is for you – now Baba." The old man came to life – breaking free of his trance all of a sudden. "This is my Pegasus; Ah! Wounded winged horse."

"These are my wings with whose help I tried foolishly, like Icarus, to reach the skies. It is yours."

His hands trembled as he opened the roll of papers in his grasp. "I tried too soon, too hastily – and I have paid the price," he said. "Now, the time is right. I have before me all you need to make my machine fly again."

I stared. Fly. What did he mean? "Are you trying to tell me this contraption can fly?" I asked. "I have no time for your ramblings. Return the papers to uncle – or burn them – I don't care. But leave me alone."

The light caught the tears that glazed his eyes. He held my hand again.

'Baba' – he said – "listen – I am telling you something you must pay heed to.

"This bike – it can fly – no, not like a plane in the skies, but through time. It is a time machine. I made it, along with your uncle – long long ago. But I was foolish, where Vinod was smart. He knew we had only begun to get it right, I couldn't wait. He wanted to work on the bike for at least ten more years; I wanted immediate fame, immediate freedom, action.

"He won. I lost. Though he thinks he lost and I won.

"One day, I stayed back on some pretext and stole the bike. When I say I stole it, I mean, I used it. I set the time and pushed it into motion.

"Chaos! Madness – worlds roared past me – I was

lost. I had only planned a trial trip. A quick journey back, a quick journey ahead — and then I'd be done. And how I'd crow to the press about what I had done!

"But none of that happened. The bike rocked violently and as we raced through the years — something snapped. Vinod had been right all along; it was too early. Before I knew what hit me the bike crashed to the floor — and I fell with the force of years rushing to meet me.

"When I awoke — it was dark. I was not in the room I had started from. Instead, I lay twisted under a sky in which every star seemed to be laughing at my plight.

"Fortunately, it was night — and I could recover the bike and limp away to shelter before I was mistaken for a tramp or a thief. I wandered the streets trying to discover where I was. That I was still in Lucknow was obvious — but the time was wrong. I had no inkling how far I had travelled or in which direction.

"I won't go into the weeks and months of agony I went through before I began to put my life together again. The loss of my family, my home — my dear wife whom I loved to distraction, the child who was to be born in a couple of months, they gnawed at me the most — rebuking me each moment for my selfishness, my insane foolishness.

"I had lost everything I had. Home and family, of course. But fame too. Without the means to go back, there was no way I could prove who I was or what I had done. Luckily for me, I realised I had not travelled far. Ten years or so. And what are ten years in the ocean of eternity? I could easily have travelled twenty or two hundred. Ten years, I consoled myself, were a chasm that could be spanned. There was hope.

"It took a lot of time, but slowly I managed to piece

my lift together again. My first move was to locate Vinod. He was my only hope — through him I could locate my wife.

"But Vinod was nowhere to be found. I located his house, and my own too — but both were occupied by strangers. No one seemed to know where Vinod had gone. Someone told me that Varsha, my wife, was dead, years ago — but there was no other information.

"I could not face any of my friends. They would not believe my story and anyway knowing my wife was dead made all contact pointless. I would rather remain unknown, anonymous — I felt.

"I did not give up my search for Vinod. Finding him could be my passport to life again. With his help, I could return in time — eke out the few years of life with Varsha — regain the happiness I had cheated myself out of.

"It took months — but I finally tracked Vinod down. I found him quite by accident — on a hunch that he had moved to his sister's home in Bombay.

"I found Vinod as changed a man as myself. I watched him from afar — before I revealed myself - and the extent of damage I had done shocked even my deadened senses. The old keen-eyed scientist was gone; the man I watched was sullen, defeated. My heart went out to him, I almost stepped up and confessed.

"Then even as I made up my mind, you came out. A lovely child. To say the least, I was surprised to see you — I did not imagine Vinod would marry and have children. But the way he turned on you, the venom he unleashed as he pushed you out of his way — the way you clung to him braving his anger, till he finally threw you off, made me reverse my impression. This was no married man with a family – this Vinod I saw was a wretched, bitter creature, with no love for anyone, anything. How even a man as embittered as Vinod could treat a child so harshly, was beyond my comprehension. But though I felt pity, though I wanted to rush out and save you – as I would have saved any child – from his anger, I remained hidden. This Vinod would not accept my confession. There was no scope for forgiveness in him. He was a man devoid of human spirit. And I know, in some way, I was responsible for it all. I will not go into the exercise that resulted in my finding a place in Vinod's large and loveless home. The shock of being a traveller lost in time had aged me enough to change my identity almost completely – and it was easy enough for me to find a job as jack of all trades. I cooked, I cleaned and wiped and kept house, I tended to your long neglected needs, feeling pity for you – motherless and so hated. No one knew what made Vinod hate you so much – his hatred of you extended to your dead mother – who must have been his wife, what the poor woman had done to deserve such hate, no one could tell – but he could not bear to hear her mentioned. It was as if she had never existed – he had removed all traces of her from the house – no photograph, not a warranty keepsake could tell anything of her – and the only evidence that a woman had ever lived here, belonged to his dead sister.

"I never lost sight of the true purpose of my stay – I was biding my time. It was quite obvious that Vinod was furiously at work on the time machine – he planned to recapture the glory that had almost been his – and I was waiting for that moment. Each time he would lock himself in his workshop – I would die a little. The anxiety that would grip my heart would eat away all patience – I was a changed man; waiting for my time to come. And once again, I would rob Vinod of his glory. Vinod's glory — that was a lost cause when faced with the prospect of my return to life, to my past!

"Ten years. Ten years I have waited, Baba — ten years that passed as ten eons. And now my time has come. Here, at last, is the key to the past — to the future."

He held out the papers. 'If you work with me on it — the machine will work again. And this time — there will be no mistake."

I deliberated for a while. The old man's tale was fantastic. If it was true — here was my chance to get even. Uncle Vinod — I could not bear to think of him as father — though if the old man was right, he was indeed my parent. My thoughts turned to his hatred of me; his lack of tolerance; and to that unseen entity, that never made its presence felt, my mother. I would vindicate her; give her the love she never had. Receive from her love she never could give. A strange plan began to form in my mind.

Kaka reached out to touch the bike — a touch so full of love that I could almost see the bike pulsating a response. "Put the findings at work," he said, "and I can go back to where I came from. Will you not do that for an old man — who has showered you with whatever love he had — whatever love you've ever known — in the long years past?"

I smiled to myself. The old man was fooling only himself — his love for me was hinged as much on motive as mine for him.

I put a stop to his tirade of words. I would do as he wished — work on the machine for him — and in return I would accept a small favour. I would use the bike first. When I told him this — his face fell. He seemed to grow older almost visibly. "You won't rob an old man of his chance at life, will you, son?" he asked – "If something goes wrong – I would never be able to get back again. I've waited all these years for only this moment – and will you delay it further? Will you bargain for a joy ride through time while my time runs out – will you be so cruel?"

My heart almost softened – but not quite. I had lived a hard enough life for me to be a shrewd bargainer. "I am not asking for much," – I said, "I won't be gone long. A day by earth time – perhaps two."

"And remember," I added – turning the final turn of the screw – "I can as easily take you and these papers to Uncle Vinod."

That did it – he started trembling violently – he had seen enough of the rash side of my nature to know I could quite as well carry out my threat. But his tenacity was super human. He begged and cajoled and bribed – but I held my right for the first chance at the bike. And finally, he gave in, as I knew he would. He had lost the battle long ago – though he did not know it then. He knew it now. With trembling hands, he handed over the papers to me. "I have everything we need," he added, and revealed to me a mesh of wires and electronic equipment in a corner. We set to work – I translating the calculations and he, applying them. It took all of four hours – but soon the wires were in place, the clips fitted in – and the bike looked ready to go.

I stepped back to admire my handiwork. Uncle Vinod – Papa – would have been proud of me, his half-taught pupil. I turned to look as Ramu Kaka.

I will never, never forget the look in his eyes. Such longing – the yearning of ten million years was locked into that glance – as he glazed at the bike. No father had looked at a long lost son with such intensity. No exile had looked at a forbidden shore with such longing. I hardened my heart once again, telling myself this was my one chance to make my life worthwhile, to experience something no man in my time had ever felt before. I strapped myself in, mindful of the old man's experiences in the past. Kaka sat stunned – disbelieving, his eyes refusing to see his creation being snatched away. He was an old fool – though if he thought I was indeed going to return in a few hours, he could think again a thousand times over. I had the eons in my grasp, and I was no fool. I would choose a time and place of my liking, consider my advantages, sample the options and decide where I would live the rest of my life. My hitherto aimless existence would be projected into a new meaningfulness. In a few moments.

I started the motors, and sat back. My eyes were fixed on the shadow on the wall – Kaka's shadow. In that moment of triumph, I could not bear to look at the fool who had let fate fool him twice in a lifetime.

Even as I watched, the shadow flickered – like a flickering flame which trembles when, it swayed, and divided itself into hazy sections – finally disappearing from view.

I realised that the room was spinning – space spun in a cloud, the wind rushed past my eyes, though even the hem of my kurta did not move in the gale. My eyes were blinded by the glare, the tearing force of time rushing by – and I pushed on the buttons – trying to make out how far I had gone – and in which direction.

Suddenly, everything stopped. The world swung back into focus. I looked around me, at a strange landscape – a copper sky, a deadened earth. This was not Bombay.

I looked at the compass – I had travelled northeast – a few latitudes, somehow the bike had set its course – or perhaps Kaka had.

I could not determine whether it was day or night – the copper sky held neither sun nor moon, there were no trees – nothing.

Squinting through the tears that still smarted in my eyes, I decoded the numbers in the timemeter. I had a brief journey – it was barely 20 years. Whether I had travelled in the past or the future – only time could tell. I set myself to take off again. A few hundred years would be a worthwhile experience. Something to talk about, if I should choose to return. And something to shock Kaka with – and uncle too – should I ever meet either of them again.

I was just about to set off the starter, when a thought struck me. Twenty years – that was just about the time I was born. Would this not be as good an opportunity as any to see the mother I had never known? To see my father as a young man – as the brilliant researcher he was before – grief-struck, before the calamity hit him, that he never forgave my mother for. It dawned on me that Uncle Vinod – my father, I reminded myself – had been wrong. It was not my mother who had wrecked his life. It was Ramu Kaka – or whatever his real name was. Friend, fellow scientist, philanderer, thief.

A rush of filial affection decided the matter for me. I could clear my mother's name, catch Kaka in the act – and perhaps one day, clear my mother and thus myself, in Uncle Vinod's eyes. Finding my mother would give me a love I never had known, and may never know – finding Ramu Kaka and preventing his deed – may win me a love I might yet know...

I was drained of all energy. Confused in time, neither in the past nor the future – in that uncertain present, I wanted to break free and find a mooring, a familiar face, a human voice that could tell me I was still in the realm of men.

The sound of voices came to my ears, almost as a shock – thought it was indeed the fastest answer to a prayer I had ever known. I looked around the grey air – it dawned on me that I was not under the sky. The copper dome I had mistaken for the firmament was a ceiling – I stood on a floor covered with some kind of covering. The voices came from without. I was safe, yet unrevealed within.

Galvanised out of my inertia, I shook off the timelessness that hung about me, unstrapped myself from the bike and set about finding my way out of the room. My first act was to hide the bike – it would not do to let it fall into anyone's hand at all – it was my only lifeline to safety, I could not let myself be caught like Ramu Kaka, lost in a strange time and place.

Bike hidden behind a mass of apparatus – I moved cautiously round the room, discovering its contours. It revealed itself to be an observatory of sorts or perhaps a work laboratory – but ill-used. That was good enough for me. I prepared to let myself out of the place.

The voices had faded – the few catchwords and phrases I had heard assured me I would be able to hide my identity sufficiently. They spoke my tongue, my jargon, I peered cautiously out from behind the heavy, unoiled door that took all my might to push open – I found myself looking down a long corridor. A rectangle of lawn on one side – and a wall with windows on the other – but before I could decide whether this was a hospital or not – the voices came back again, and I withdrew.

Young forms passed me, casting colourful shadows where I stood, concealed behind the door. I looked out, to see better and caught sight of two young men – one of my

A BICYCLE FOR TWO

own age, perhaps, dressed in casual clothes and two girls, they looked very young but carried themselves with a poise that only came with maturity and practice.

I watched them walk – though float was a better word to describe the way one of the girls moved – and then they turned into a door against the wall and were out of sight. I stood there, pondering over my next move.

***

Time has lost its meaning since I landed in this place. Two days I know have passed since I first arrived in this time – and what eventful days they have been! I discovered soon enough I was in the university campus – that I could fit in quite easily into the set up – I decided to hang around for a while, for the fun of it, and then move on. I soon gave up my idealistic idea of finding my mother – I had no chance – not knowing how she looked or where she was, there was no point in spending precious time looking for her. Besides, I had Naomi to think about. Naomi. Would she be a port in the sea of my travels through time – or a permanent anchor? I knew it was more likely to be the former; there was no reason to let myself be dazzled even before I had sampled the variety time would be able to offer me – I was obsessed with her. She had taken total hold of my 22-year-old senses.

But how I wander. I must explain that Naomi had made me decide to quite forget my original intention – of looking for my mother. Her very obvious attraction was too strong a force to ignore – and my intense longing to meet my mother evaporated before its power. If it was some womanly warmth I was looking for – Naomi would be more than adequate.

Classes were quite chaotic, it did not take me long to fit in — I just meandered about and attended the classes Naomi attended, even proving a good student and it was not long before the teachers accepted my presence. I suppose I was one of the few serious ones, and that was reason enough to blind them to the circumstances of my sudden appearance, halfway through the second term.

My seriousness in studies had an ulterior motive. It got me Naomi's attention — and it was not long before, using my extraordinary precociousness in mathematics to advantage, I had managed to get on to the business of knowing her better. Soon, I was flirting a little, more serious at times — a few months more and I would have the girl eating out of my hand. Of course I had Ranjan, her friend and my rival to contend with — he was always lurking around her, but Ranjan's battle was lost for him. He did not have my experience — he did not have time on his side. Time gave me knowledge, a sense of perspective that added a quiet deliberation to my actions — and I realised, made me an object of fascination for Naomi. It would not be long — it wasn't long before studies were relegated to being a mere backdrop to the more colourful aspects of the growing relationship between Naomi and me.

The strangest things happen without any apparent warning. Today in the English class, Nila Bhagwat fainted in the middle of a sentence. I haven't spoken of Nila Bhagwat before only because I have been so blinded by Naomi's presence, that I have no eyes for anyone else.

Nila Bhagwat is one of our lecturers — there is something in her that is both attractive and putting off. She carries herself, despite her pregnancy, in an ethereal manner, as if she is above mortal acts like walking on mere ground. Yet there is much of an air of tragedy about her

– others, especially the callow young men in her class find it irresistible – but I find it very putting off. Tragedy queens are best viewed from a distance, unless you want your shoulder loaded to the bone.

Naomi told me that I was being harsh on Nila. She was quite a nice person, still coming to terms with the fact that her husband had deserted her, a few months ago.

Nobody knew why – but rumour spoke in many tongues. People said he had absconded with another woman; others said it was she who had caused him to leave – when he discovered her infidelity – but the fact remained that he had just upped and left. While she was here in college teaching the class about Hamlet and his 'to be or not to be,' he made his decision and left. Nila had stayed home, distraught for two days. Then she came back, wearing a watery smile and a newly acquired queen of tragedy look. After all, she had to support herself, and run her home. And there was the baby. The college women were totally on her side though that did not stop the rumours.

So, when Nila dropped like a heap of unwashed clothes in class, there was pandemonium. The college doctor was summoned and looking at her, insisted she should be taken home. Rest was imperative – that was all we heard. What was wrong with Nila – we could only guess of course – the guesses ranged from a threatened suicide to a heart problem arising from the shock of desertion. The net result was, however, that our English classes were free; and Naomi had me to listen to instead – and, when I moved on from explaining Hamlet to talking about the beauty of her eyes, as I often did – Naomi did not really seem to mind. Life was full to the brim.

Distractions seem inevitable. But as the days went past, the fact became increasingly clear that there was a purpose to my being in this time and place, at this point in my life. Naomi was one of them – she textured my life completely, her soft giving nature, her total dependence on me for everything, coloured my own perceptions. I lost a lot of my previous detachment, and often found myself almost believing myself to be a permanent resident of this time. It was not difficult. Confined as I was due to a lack of funds, to the campus and observatory, which I had made my home – with Naomi as the main object around which my life currently revolved – it gave me a sense of security I had never felt in all the years of my existence before. Naomi's belief in my penniless state resulting from my being a self-made man still on the make – helped tide over any crisis that could arise out of my lack of funds. She tended all my needs – emotional and real. I consoled myself that one day, I would make it up to her. Besides that vague thought – I did not care to think. This was getting more complicated than I could cope with.

Even as I struggled to come to terms with my inertia, my unwillingness to leave this time sphere and resume my adventure – something happened to shock me out of my becalmed state.

The exams were approaching. Despite ourselves, Naomi and I found we were caught up in exam fever. There was first the need to prove ourselves worthy of each other – then to move ahead with the mainstream. Being left behind would suit neither my scheme of things – nor – Naomi's and so we applied ourselves to our studies spending hours making up for those we had wasted. Thus, it was imperative to get lost notes, and model papers – all the crutches other students had already acquired to equip themselves for the long race ahead. Naomi took upon herself the task of visiting the lecturers at their chambers, making up for the lost time by absorbing what she could of their teaching. Her soft ways ensured she was not turned away and she often came back with wads of notes which she would share with me.

One such visit took us to Nila Bhagwat's house. I had not seen much of Lucknow (which was the city I had landed in I discovered) – had not ventured out of the campus for fear of complicating my life – but I was persuaded to accompany Naomi.

Nothing, but nothing had prepared me for what I discovered there.

Quite accidentally, with the casualness of a film clip revealing a secret, my life tumbled into a heap. Everything I thought I was, I wasn't. Not self-possessed, not man of the world; my cynicism, the thick veneer of sophisticated detachment that I put on before everyone except Naomi, cracked beyond repair. In one swift moment, I was reduced to a dithering, sentimental idiot. Revealed for what I was. A tool of time, a creature of no consequence. My eye took the photograph in quite casually – Nila Bhagwat stood in the centre, with two men on either side. Something about her smile, the freshness of her young beauty – attracted my gaze. I went nearer – and caught Uncle Vinod looking back at me from the picture.

To say my knees shook would be a lie. I felt time hit me with the force of a sledge hammer, knocking my breath away. Uncle Vinod and Nila Bhagwat – the other man in the picture – could it be Ramu Kaka? I rose shakily – but I could not be sure. But Uncle Vinod – the same gaze, the same slick of his hair across his forehead. There was no doubt. I stumbled out of there, forgetting Naomi, forgetting everything but my need, desperate need for solitude. Safety.

Later, much later, in the quiet of my observatory, I came out of my stupor. Nila Bhagwat — Uncle Vinod — faces, names had run a merry-go-round in my mind till I had gone dizzy and blacked out. But now it was clear. Nila was Uncle Vinod's wife — and — Ramu Kaka had said I was Uncle Vinod's son — then — certainly — Nila was my mother.

For some reason, the knowledge hit me hard. I felt a sneaking guilt — as if I had been Oedipus caught seducing his mother.

The third thought struck me with even greater force. If Nila was my mother, then the child she carried — that was me!

I was trapped indeed. Foolish, foolish man to ever think he can take hold of time, and change things around. I had stopped here in Lucknow. Hoping to find my mother, hoping to find the love I had never received. But now finding her, despite all odds — how could I reveal myself to her, and find that love? It would be foolish — any relationship between Nila and me would be misconstrued — she was still young and almost beautiful, I was one of her students, many of whom were smitten by her to a point of foolish infatuation. No. It would not be. Even if I revealed myself to Nila and she believed me — there was no way for us to further this relationship. I made up my mind, even as I heard Naomi's soft voice enquire from outside if I was there.

I would wait and watch, tending over Nila in whatever way I could. I would vindicate her name, so when I went back to the future, my real present, I could prove to Uncle Vinod, his wife was blameless. I knew now, Uncle Vinod's hatred of Nila stemmed from suspicion — he probably believed her to be unfaithful, whereas Nila, I knew now, could only be blameless. Once I proved this, uncle would look on me with less hatred too. And maybe I would earn his love by giving his mind release from the doubts that had tortured him through the years.

Slowly, with great caution, I made arrangements to ensure Nila, my mother, was cared for. I awoke Naomi's protective instincts, speaking of how the poor woman must be managing alone in that house, ill and untended to except by the servants. Naomi, unsuspecting, rose to the bait – of breaking the cocoon she had surrounded herself in. Bridging the teacher-pupil gap, Naomi with characteristic grace and softness, found a cause to help, and it was not long before Nila responded to her overtures. The bonds of friendship strengthened between the two women who mattered most in my life. I watched them grow, knowing myself helpless to do more. The knowledge that the moment of my birth would cut short my mother's life was a weight that tortured my mind. But there was nothing I could do but watch helplessly.

I watched as helplessly on the night that Naomi rushed Nila to the hospital. I sat with Naomi outside the door, her anxiety was only tinged with the fear of the unknown, mine was a surety. What I felt was beyond anxiety. It was the dreadful knowledge that I was witnessing my mother's last hours; and had yet no way of letting her know who I was, or how much I cared.

Somewhere in the mists of half sleep weighed by the deadening certainty of disaster, I caught sight of a familiar figure. Something in the way the shoulders stooped, that lock of hair – yes it was Uncle Vinod. I rose with a start – but he still stood there waiting.

I ran to him, to welcome him back, to tell him to make peace with his blameless wife, while there was yet time.

Time — the word brought me back to my defeated state — a traveller without moorings. I was as good as invisible. I sent Naomi home — I would wait in her stead, I told her, call her should any emergency arise. She left unwillingly. But as I watched her go, I felt relief. Uncle Vinod and I had reason to be there — and I hoped still, for a chance to reveal myself. Naomi was best out of this mess.

What happened soon after, I will never be able to tell. I can only guess. Deep inside the hospital, my mother gave birth to me. That I know for sure or I wouldn't be here. I noted down the exact date — so that I know my birth date for the first time.

I went out to phone Naomi — when I heard the nurses announcing the birth — my mind was in turmoil — that the death of a mother I had never really known should disturb me so much was unbelievable. Yet, I know I felt responsible in some way. My life had caused her death.

By the time Naomi came, it was dawn. I sat outside the hospital waiting for her, watching the beginning of day. The birth of day, I thought, put an end to darkness — why was my birth then steeped in darkness?

Naomi came, flushed with excitement. Was all well? Was Nila safe? Was it a boy or girl?

I knew all the answers, but I had no answers to any of her questions, she ran lightly up the steps — I followed with heavy tread — fearful of what I knew we would find.

The nurse who met us was impassive. No, we could not meet Nila — she was still sedated. The baby was well. A boy. More than that, she would not say.

Naomi breathed a prayer in response — I was flummoxed. Nila was sleeping. Not dead? I was told she died at the moment of my birth — how then could she still be alive? There was some mistake – either the nurse had not realised Nila was dead – or that child was not me; and Nila was not my mother after all. I longed to take Naomi into my confidence – to have someone with whom I could thrash the whole thing out with. Wishful thinking. I might as well expect the moon to shine by day.

Anyway, for the present, my main problem was to wait till I could see Nila, or be sure of her condition – and to wait without showing an impatience for which I could not offer any explanation.

We bided our time, Naomi and I, at the hospital – walking through the corridors, imbibing the atmosphere of the place. All of this only quickened my anxiety, till I could bear it no more – I grabbed Naomi by the hand, and ran out of the place, till I breathed fresh air in great gulps.

Hours later, returning to the ward where Nila lay, my mind was seized by dread again. I did not know what to expect, but whatever it was – it would not be good.

What we found staggered me beyond belief. There was no Nila–dead or alive. No child. Nothing.

"Dr. Vinod insisted on moving them to a better, private hospital – so I had to discharge them," the matron said. "He was so angry – I don't know why, we are a clean, decent hospital – but big men have their preferences." And that was the end of that.

"Dr. Vinod, that is Nila's husband," I cried out to Naomi. "Why did he return suddenly? Why did he disappear in the first place? There's a mystery."

Naomi sat down, her calm face furrowed with doubt. Dr. Vinod – she repeated. Dr. Vinod is Nila's husband? Come on, silly, you've got your facts mixed up. He's only her husband's friend and fellow scientist.

Nila's husband is Dr. Bhagwat—who disappeared months ago. And Vinod is only doing the right thing.

I needed to flee again – this was too much; this fresh revelation had knocked the world from over my head. Uncle Vinod – Dr. Bhagwat – who was Dr. Bhagwat? – the man in the photograph, had I seen him carefully – was he indeed Ramu Kaka?

Yes, of course, Ramu Kaka had taken a time machine ride, leaving behind a wife and an unborn child. Me! Nila's husband had disappeared. No one but I knew why – he had not run away with another woman—he had travelled through time—lost himself in it.

And here I was – a time traveller – ferreting out truths I should never have known. Never could come face to face with.

I put my head in my hands, and much to Naomi's consternation, sobbed uncontrollably!

There was nothing to do but go back. Back to where I belong. My search for my mother drew a blank. Dr. Vinod had taken her and her child to god knows where. I knew where my search would finally lead me – to Bombay, to Uncle Vinod's place with me growing up as the scapegoat on whom he could wreak his frustrations, his anger against Dr. Bhagwat's treachery. But he was still in Bombay. I checked that out, of course, before I gave up hope.

I sat down and took stock of the findings in front of me. I had found my mother – and lost her – but I knew she was not dead. If she had survived the birth – and Uncle Vinod insisted she hadn't – there was cause to believe she was still alive. Though where? Only time – I smiled a wry smile at the unintended irony – would tell!

A BICYCLE FOR TWO

I had found my father – and for him, I would find his wife. That was a plus point. I could undo all the hate and contempt I had unleashed on Kaka, by telling him his wife was alive. Even traceable.

I had found Naomi – was about to lose her.

There was no point in living in the past. Nor of going back to the present, if it meant losing Naomi. Would I ever find her in the present? Would she know me?

I pondered over all these facts while I sat in Naomi's room. She would not let me be, she knew I was passing through some uncontrollable crisis, and though she refrained from questioning me – she made sure she was always near me. A steadfast supporting presence. As if she had heard my thoughts, Naomi stood at my side – smiling at my worried face. She reached out and in a typical gesture, smoothed out the furrows on my forehead one by one. "Don't worry so much," she said. "We can solve anything together. Why don't you tell me what it is?"

I almost told her then – but the fear of losing her was what kept me silent. But somewhere, my mind was made up. I wouldn't tell her. I'd show her, and she'd be glad. Unafraid.

It took me a week to take down all the details; Nila's address, the exact dates, everything. And to persuade Naomi to pack. She was to trust me – I wouldn't say more.

"Do you want to trust me?" I asked. She smiled a reply. "Then do so," I added. "Pack a light bag of everything most precious to you. And leave no clues – you are going on a journey which you may never return from." She looked afraid, then smiled, "As long as we are together," she said, thinking perhaps that I was joking, That was my hope. We'd have great times together, we would. I began to feel light-hearted for the first time in a long, long time.

The ride back was much worse than the earlier one. The bike was not meant for two people – not two people travelling through space anyway. Naomi thought for a while that I was some kind of a nut, riding doubles on a bike in an observatory – but when the thing got into motion, she let out a shrill, high shriek of distilled terror, and then sat so quiet I had to check if she was still there. Only her arms wound tight around my middle proved she was – I hadn't lost my pillion rider on the way. The lights came back slowly and the rush of time slowed perceptibly as the time control showed we were approaching our destination. I mentally tried to prepare Naomi for the landing ahead – but there was no way I could make myself heard over the roar, so I put my hand over hers to reassure her that we were safe and together. The light turned mellow and then evened out and soon the spinning stopped, I heaved a sigh of relief. We were safe.

Surveying the room, I realised nothing much had changed. Kaka was still living there. And even as I moved to the door, he came running in.

"I knew it – I knew from the sound that you had come – how I have waited for..." he touched my hands and face, as if unsure I had indeed come back. I felt a rush of emotion as I watched this pitiful performance. I had been harsh indeed, upon this poor old man, who was my father.

Kaka noticed Naomi – and stopped to stare. "You brought her back!" – he whispered – "from how far? Will she survive the change – what have you done?"

I soothed him, telling him Naomi and I could not possibly live in two different worlds, especially since we were getting married.

Kaka stared some more. All this was beyond his understanding. But I had more to tell him. His concern, however, overcame his curiosity. As he wandered around the room, trying to put together something for us to eat and drink, he worried about Naomi. About how we would live. And he worried most about Uncle Vinod. "How will your father react to this?" he asked repeatedly.

It was time for the truth – I told him all I knew – Naomi listened intently, a child listening to a fairy tale. I watched her from a corner of my eyes, half afraid of shock or horror or recoil. But she was calm.

Kaka, on the other hand, almost swooned when I mentioned Nila Bhagwat – and by the time I told him who I was and that she was alive – he was barely alive himself.

"Vinod" – he said – "Vinod did that to both of you – I will show him. I will ask him where she is – he must, he must tell me." Then, he looked at me with an unbounding love in his eyes. "Son," he said, "You are mine, and I've lived with you for ten years without knowing it."

He got up—wary of touching me—past experience had proved often enough my impatience with his expressions of love – and he did not want to risk irritating me. I moved closer and put a hand on his shoulder.

"Father" – the word came with difficulty; "forgive me for all my past sins." He smiled a tearful smile and patted me on the back and started off, "I must find Nila – Vinod must answer for this," he said. I watched him go, a bent, shaken man, unable to cope with the discoveries I had uncovered for him – then a thought occurred to me.

"Father – Kaka – Ramu Kaka," – I stopped him, listen – I have a plan."

I told him the plan. "What use is it finding Nila?" I asked – "She may be old, sick, wretched. And that will make both of you alone and wretched in this world."

He looked at me uncomprehending, wondering what could make me sound so cruel. Even Naomi looked startled.

I hastened to explain. "Kaka, you can get back all the years you lost," I said. "Go back in time, it will be easier to find her there and even if it is too late to find me – the years in between, the twenty years of your life together that time displaced can be recaptured, relived."

It took persuasion, especially since emotion made me clumsy with words. But I finally put it across, and Kaka gave up his idea of accosting Vinod, and decided instead to go back to where he had come from.

We strapped him into place—and bid our farewells. I felt a lingering sorrow over his going – this man whom I had known so well, and yet so little. Kaka smiled a dim farewell and spun out into timelessness with a rush of cold air.

Naomi and I set out, to seek our lives together.

***

Years have passed. Uncle Vinod died soon after and I inherited his house and lands, as also his estate. Naomi and I live a life of such peace and togetherness, it has made the journey more than worthwhile. Often on balmy evenings, we wonder whether Kaka and Nila too did find one another – and whether they are enjoying the togetherness we have. Sometimes Naomi talks of meeting them, suggests I complete Uncle Vinod's time machine and set out to search for them, but I am wary of making the kind of mistake Kaka made; and finding myself losing all I have gained.

On occasions, Naomi and I drive through town on my motor bike – it is our way of reliving the bike ride that has resulted in our present.

Today is one of those days. As we turn into the highway, the level crossing closes. And the local train goes past.

For a fleeting moment, Naomi tenses behind me. "Look – look quickly," she says, guiding my look with a pointing finger.

I look in the direction she points in, and my gaze catches sight of – yes – it's – no, it couldn't be, yet it is – Ramu Kaka standing by the door. And even the glimpse is enough to tell me that time has restored him, cast away the years that had gathered around him, weighing his shoulders. I get a sight of Nila, as the carriage moves out of sight, it convinces me that it is she who stands by his side.

Naomi and I stare at each other. They are back. They have found each other – and made the journey back – thoughts careen with the speed of time, as we stare at each other.

Then in unison, almost, Naomi and I shout, "Churchgate the train's headed there – Let's catch them…."

And we are off in a whoosh, searching for our pasts, our future.

9

BEYOND THE LOOKING GLASS

MINI STEPPED INTO the darkening room. The mirror gleamed shyly in the half light. Mini's eyes shone back. It was an old game, and of her own making.

Slowly, she moved closer to the oval shape that held her image. Surely, she placed one small sweet hand over another, finger against finger, thumb to thumb. Next, forehead to forehead. "Now," she whispered. "Now." The command hazed and blurred against the smooth glass...

***

Sometimes, I don't know whether I sleep or wake. Whether the shrill sudden cries of children playing outside come from the past, or really are. I can hear them now – voices rising sporadically over the swish of the palm leaves that the summer winds stirs. But I know it cannot be. There are no children any more. They have either grown up, or died, or been sent away to play elsewhere – where the sound of their laughter will not mock a dying woman's pain.

Grandma. Grandma. The voice strokes my consciousness, so softly that I mistake it for another dream. But the warm hand that slips into my cold one is real. And I remember. Mini. Little six-year-old Mini. Ever since she has come into my life, there is a new purpose behind my living. A definite reason.

Grandma, I brought you this. Her eyes are black with excitement, and she lifts my hand to show me the yellow flower she has placed between my fingers. Smell it, grandma, it smells so sweet. She nuzzles into the petals, inhaling their fragrance on my behalf. Mini, I am learning to live again. Through you. You don't realise what a blessing you are to a childless, old woman like me.

Surprisingly, Mini's coming was a deciding factor. Now, after years of living in fear, in pain, in dread, I am at ease. I am prepared. I can look death in the face and smile.

After living seventy years in this house, in this decrepit, crumbling ruin that will not yet forego its grandeur, I could not face the idea of living, even in death, anywhere else. Even now, even with my failing sight, on quiet moonlit nights — when Jayam and the night nurse have finally ceased their pointless ministrations and fallen noisily asleep; flitting in through the dusty stained glass panes, I can see the old magic again. The ivory-inlaid swing nods gently in the moonlight on such nights; the Venetian glass shades tinkle in the night breeze. I can even smell the fragrance of the long forgotten flower beds…

"Grandma, don't fall asleep again. Mother will soon come to fetch me. I don't have much time." Mini's breath fanned my ear, redolent of the gardens beyond my door. "Yes," I say, some forgotten light illuminating my grey-ringed eyes. "I mustn't sleep; now that you are here."

We play a game, Mini and I. I've designated her my eyes and ears; her feet are mine as are her hands; and through her I roam the corridors of my beloved home again.

Through her, I feel once again the cool marble beneath my feet, the warm touch of the cement columns against my cheek. Her fingers are mine as they slide over the crystal door knobs, as they linger to caress the shoulder of the marble Venus that Jayam has locked safely out of sight.

And in her awakening sense of wonder, I catch sight of my own wonderment, seventy years ago, when I first entered this great house as a girl bride.

"Where shall I go today?" Mini's excitement ignited my memory and I remembered the old room in the west wing upstairs. There is a room at the end of the long corridor on top, I told her, it has no lock. But no one had entered it for years. No one dared to but me, and it's been a year since I could walk. Will you go there today?

"Why Grandma, why are they scared?" she asked. And I told her of the horsehair four-poster and the dreams anyone who slept on it had – ever since Jayam's husband died in it during an afternoon nap. Of the rows and rows of books on criminology that lined the shelves for years after his death, Jayam would not let anyone touch them, or dispose of them. I told her too of my own meetings with the spirits that walked in life, chary of leaving. And as I spoke, Mini's eyes grew round and black with suppressed excitement.

The grandfather clock struck three. By five, her mother would come for her, to take her home, to homework and all the chores a little girl must do. And though the woman is in my pay, though it was I who told Jayam to select her husband out of a dozen applicants for the caretaker's post, she has scant respect for me. She would stop Mini from meeting me if she dared – but her husband is a greedy man, and ever since the day I gave Mini one of my old gold rings as a gift, he will not heed his wife's dislike of me.

"Rush, child," I said, "and don't be afraid. And don't linger too long, either. You must tell me what you see, before you go."

There was no time for that, though. Mini lingered, fascinated beyond her control... Unerringly, her eye had spotted the wooden cupboard, its dark ebony frame holding the oval mirror, and unerringly she had divined its real nature.

The rest of the house lost its magic for Mini. Every afternoon, she would spend hours in the room on the west. My favourite hiding place for years now had a new tenant.

Each time she'd lie on the couch and sleep, I'd dream her dreams as I lay on my bed, a staircase and five rooms away. I knew they were no dreams, for how could Mini have known all she told me about the spirits who spoke to her while she slept?

And each day, before she returned, she would open the cupboard and look at the dark, bare shelves within. And hear the voices whisper. And I would translate the dreams, the whispers into tales; tell her of the past and its people and all they had meant to me, to this house. Mini was a treasure. Through her, I could tryst with my entire family again.

Of course, no one knew. Not Jayam, who wondered what Mini found to talk with me; not the nurse, who would try to shoo her away. Mini would mimic the woman's scolding voice. "Go away, let the poor lady rest in peace. Go, go..." As if you are already dead, Grandma, she'd laugh, and conceal her mouth to smother the sounds of her mirth. No one knew, thankfully, of Mini's trysts with my past.

Then it came. The whisper from the cupboard spoke

it out clearly. Mini enunciated the words carefully. "Come, it said, Grandma. It clearly called out to me. I felt a cold breeze touch me, and I closed the door and came out. Grandma, for the first time I was afraid."

I soothed her, smiling despite my fear. For the call had not been for Mini, but for me. My time had come. I was being warned – being given notice so I could prepare.

I had to be gentle. "Mini," I said, "the voice was not for you. It was calling me. It is time for me to join the voices in the cupboard."

Mini stared at me as if I had suddenly started talking gibberish. "But you can't walk, Grandma, how will you climb those stairs?"

The child's game had ended. It was time to turn serious. But how much could I explain to a six-year-old? I kept my silence, and made my own arrangements.

Quietly, I made a will, calling two of the garden boys to witness. I left the house to Mini in trust; nothing was to be changed or broken or destroyed after my death. It would all have to be looked after exactly as it was now, till Mini could take care of it herself. Her parents would, of course, continue to live in the outhouse, but Mini would have access to the house whenever she pleased. I hid the will in the box under my bed – they would open it soon enough after my death – and the will would be safe then. There was no point in telling Jayam now; I would have to face her hysterics. Of course, I had made provisions for Jayam, she would have enough to settle elsewhere; and would probably be glad to get rid of the responsibility of this house. But to try telling her that was foolish. And frankly, quite beyond my capacity.

"Mini," I said one afternoon, a few days later, "will

you walk through the corridors today for me?" She looked somewhat disappointed. "Just for today," I said, "Tomorrow, you can go upstairs again."

But when she had walked the marble floor and passed under the bead curtains, I made her explore the rooms next to mine. Bouncing on the springy sofas, lounging on the unpainted wooden grandchair – it was like being a girl again. I delighted in every movement she made; willed her to linger, pause, absorb. My bones would ache at night, but time was precious. Anyway, release was near.

I tutored her carefully now, before I let her enter the room at the west end, upstairs, once more. There was no time to lose. If I left it undone, my entire life would go wasted.

"Mini," I whispered, because Jayam sat on the swing nearby, embroidering bright purple daisies on a kitchen towel.

"Mini, listen carefully. When I am not here, you must look for me behind the mirror. Not in the cupboard, really, but in the mirror." Her eyes questioned me – but I stopped her words before they could voice themselves. "I know," I said, "all the voices in the cupboard – they live behind the mirror, I've been there."

"No," I added, hearing her question even as it snaked through her brain, "no, you must not look now, not till I am gone. I am not going away really, just going where no one can see me. No one, except you. Understand?"

Mini did not understand. But she would. When the time came, my Mini would be exactly right. I knew it, because I would make it so.

"Go now," I whispered, urgently now, "Go and explore the room – listen to the voices. But," my earnestness made me grip her hand so hard she winced, "do not look behind the mirror. Not yet."

When the time came, I would guide Mini to the mirror, and she would learn to see; and see to find. And finding, we would be one again. One spirit, in one frame; my girl mind blending with hers, my emaciated body happily disposed of, exchanged for hers. It would be a perfect meeting of minds, I knew that — for Mini's spirit is my own, and I have already made her mind mine. And by ensuring that she gets free access to my home, I am ensured of my future; hers too.

In the long afternoons, I will walk the corridors again; swing gaily on the ivory-embedded swings, stop to fondle a marble shoulder. The fingers that touch will be mine, and Mini's; the breeze will touch her hair and I will breathe in the scent of flowers.

Then, as the light fades, and the night comes in, and it is time to rest, I will leave Mini to her ordinary life as daughter and schoolgirl, return her to the outhouse and its world of books and chores.

Already Mini is aware of all this — for the voices are speaking for me. Telling her, as she stands entranced before the dark shelves of the wooden cabinet, what she must do. And I know she'll approve. After all, she loves me as much as I love her; and both of us love this house too.

When Mini came back, I was sure. Her eyes shone with an understanding far beyond her years, "Grandma," she said; and we both smiled.

I lay down to sleep that night, with ether in my heart. Even the pain was stilled by the singing in my soul. "Come — now. Now." The command hazed and blurred and blended into the warm night air.

10

DIWALI PROMISE

"WAKE UP KALAVATI. It is Diwali today. We'll get lots and lots to eat today..."

Rough hands... it must be Rama waking me. She is the one who always thinks of food. Diwali today... Suddenly I am awake. The sun is hot on my pillow. I know the iron rods of my bed will be hot if I touch them — they always heat up by the middle of the morning even in winter — and it is only October and still quite warm. Diwali, my mind says — and repeats — Diwali, Diwali. Today *aie* will come to take me home.

How lovely to have a mother. No one else in this place has one. Of course Kiran has a father and Raja had a stepmother who often visits her, but no one has a real one. I do! Am I not lucky? And, yet, I am an orphan. Why else would I be living in an *anathalaya?*

Aie... the word has such a lovely sound. *A-i-e*, I repeat the word, breaking it into two sounds, the longer to stay with it. When will it become dark and *aie* come?

The bell is ringing — time for food already? No time for a bath, I haven't even got out my washed frock yet. I must wash my face and fix my hair to look combed before

DIWALI PROMISE

I run down, or *maushi* will scold me for being untidy. "Aren't you coming?" Rama's voice again. "Yes, I am!" I put on my frock over the petticoat I sleep in, and rush downstairs. The line must be already formed and if I am last, I won't get enough.

It is not food-time. Some women have come with sweets. "*Jalebis* and *sheera*," Rama says excitedly, "I told you we will eat well today," she adds. Little Rahul is sitting at the beginning of the line holding his bowl up. How sweet he looks – just like the photo of Krishna *bhagwan* in *maushi's* room. Only the pot in the photo is full of curds.

I do not hold my plate up. I do not even look up when the *jalebi* lands in my plate. Somehow, I feel sad whenever we are given such food to eat. The *jalebi* smells lovely, it is sticky and sweet. But I will not lick my fingers after eating it. What a lovely sari the lady who put the *jalebi* in my plate is wearing. I have never seen such colours – I don't even know their names. My frock is brown now, it was blue when I got it last year. I love blue. Hate brown.

Aie – will she be eating *jalebis* today? What will she be cooking? Last year, she had brought *sheera* and *pedas* for me. How delicious they were – though the *pedas* were not sweet enough. What will *aie* bring this year? No, she will not bring anything, for I will be going back with her. I will eat at home tonight. Home, my home. If *maushi* will allow. But *maushi* will say yes; after all, *aie* is my own mother.

I don't feel like playing. *Maushi* has a basket of crackers in her room. Everyone else is excited about them. I do not feel anything. Last year, I had burst many crackers, all the little girls had come to me to burst their crackers because I am never afraid. But this year I feel nothing. But I cannot think of anything except wondering when it will be night; for at night, *aie* will come. I will go home.

"Kalavati, *maushi* wants you." *Didi* who looks after the babies, is calling me. *Didi* is very kind-hearted. Last week, when one of the babies, the one who was found in the dustbin, was very sick, she cried a lot over it. Today, *didi* looks happy in a new sari.

Maushi smiles when I enter... not an angry smile which means a lecture is coming, but a pleasant smile. Maybe she is going to talk about *aie*, and say that I am to go home today.

"Sit down," she says, "I want to talk to you." And continues... "Listen, Kalavati, you are a grown-up girl now, you are almost 13. So I thought I should ask you before I decide for you. Do you remember the lady who often visits us, usually wearing a white sari?" I nod. This is something different. Nothing to do with *aie*, I want to get up and go away. "That lady is Smt. Shukla," *maushi* continues. I remember now. Nice woman, always smiling. She's something called a social worker. And she actually touches us and lets the babies hold her sari or play with her fingers, unlike the other women who come with presents and food. They will say "how sweet," and "how nice" – but when the babies reach out to touch their sari edges, they move a step backwards, out of their reach. Smt. Shukla is not like that but she never brings us anything.

"Smt. Shukla is a widow with no children," *maushi* goes on. That explains the white sari. So, people who don't live in *anathalayas* are also lonely. "Listen carefully," *maushi* says, "she wants to adopt someone who will give her company. She does not want a baby or a young child, she wants a 10 or 12-year-old girl who will be a friend and companion. Like a daughter. I was thinking of you. Would you like to live in a nice house with her?"

I look up at *maushi*. "But I have to go home with *aie*"

— I say. *Maushi* stares at me. Is she looking strict? Or sad?

"Kalavati — your *aie* cannot take you home. Even if she does, she cannot afford to keep you. See? She has three young children to look after. Your step-brother and sisters. And your step-father cannot look after one more person. He will not allow you to go home."

"But"... I begin. *Maushi* interrupts me. "You will be happy with Smt. Shukla. Your *aie* lives in a hut. She has her own family to look after; you will have a hard life with her. Smt. Shukla is alone and has enough money to send you to a better school, buy you good clothes. Besides, she is lonely. Think it over and say yes."

Aie... I will not be able to live with you. I look at the three crackers that I have kept in my pocket to give my brother and sisters. Will I not be able to present them after all?

It is not good to cry on Diwali. Lakshmi *deviji* will be angry. And *maushi* will be angry too if she sees me.

It is already time for the lights. "Kalavati, help me light the lamps and get Meena and Leela with you," *didi* says.

Aie should have come by now — I have dropped oil on my frock.

Aie — she looks tired as she comes walking up. She has a bag in her hand. So, she will not take me home, or why will she bring sweets? *Aie* can I come home with you?

She smiles. What does her smile mean? Everyone smiles at me — and every smile means something. But what does *aie's* smile mean? I have known you for only two years and have met you only four times. I do not know what your smile means. Does it mean Ramteke, your husband, will let me come home? Does it mean he has agreed to accept me as his child too? Or has he beat you again like you said he did when you first told him about me, your child with no father? *Aie* am I going to be an orphan again?

Aie does not reply. She cannot hear my unasked questions. "I have brought *sheera* and *chivada* for you, Kala," she says. Then slowly, "He says I can bring you home – but only if you promise to help him run the house by earning something."

My home! I will have to give up school. My lovely books and all the stories they tell me. I will have to work. Will *maushi* agree? Or will she say I must go to Smt. Shukla? No, *aie*, I will make her agree – if not today – soon. I will spend at least next Diwali at home.

Suddenly the *deepas* seem like little stars. And I am very hungry. I cling to *aie* and hear myself crying. It is not good to cry on Diwali *puja*.

11
SMOKE RINGS

I STILL REMEMBER those evenings in Madurai. I was young then, barely 13; and Uncle Viren was the entire reason for my existence. My life revolved around him. Uncle Viren was not really my uncle — he was a friend of my uncle, but lived with him as a paying guest. And I met him while we, my mother and brother and I, were visiting my uncle at Madurai.

What evenings those were! We'd sit high up on the terrace, watching the birds in the sky. I'd skip around — I used to skip around a lot those days, you had to pay me to sit still, mother used to say — and I'd run around from one end of the terrace to the other and pretend to lean down and watch the traffic below. In truth, I was watching Uncle Viren all the time — and hoping he'd let go of his calm and stop blowing smoke rings long enough to worry about my tipping over the wall and falling; and run to stop me. He'd have to hold my arms then — and if I struggled a bit, maybe he'd have to hold me close.

But Uncle Viren never stopped blowing smoke rings. He went up to the terrace to smoke — at 26, he was not allowed to smoke in front of my grandfather and mother

— and so he spent his evenings out of sight on the terrace smoking. I spent my evenings there — only to be with him.

We were friends — of a kind — Uncle Viren and I. He could not have but guessed at my infatuation — I see that now. And it must have given him a strange kind of a thrill. That is probably why, at times, when I teased him too far — running circles around him or trying to hide his cigarettes, he'd suddenly reach out and hold my hands tight — and stare at me long. Not longingly — just long. And very steadily. Till I dropped my eyes and the laughter caught in my throat. Then he'd let me go — bend his head, to light another cigarette. Beyond that — nothing. Except in my dreams, of course. But that is another story.

I loved Uncle Viren for his looks. Dreamy, poetic. Like Keats, I thought, or Shelley — as I wandered pale and sadly, on my way back from school, when I returned to Patna where I lived. Uncle Viren could easily get T.B. from all that smoking — and he'd sit etched against the darkening sky, while the sea breeze blew the trees into graceful curves, looking paler and paler by the day, and coughing heavily once in a while, then stopping to murmur my name, before he dragged at his cigarette. That was the stuff my dreams were made of. Uncle Viren would die, languishing for me, because he did not speak of his love, and I had given up my life in despair. Dreams. I had plenty and more, and of every possible kind. Most of them were, of course, about Uncle Viren.

When he was not on the terrace, Uncle Viren was working in the income tax office. Some junior officer — but I knew nothing of his life by day. To me, he existed the moment he stepped out of his room, changed into a bush shirt and loose pants, his pocket bulging suspiciously with two or three packets of cigarettes, as he headed for the stairs to the terrace.

The terrace was two floors up. My mother could not climb to the first floor, my uncle could and would – but he seldom bothered to come to the terrace. And so Uncle Viren and I could spend our evening trading jokes, teasing each other and watching the birds. All while I was watching him and spinning my never ending dreams. Dreams – I look at Viren today and wonder what caused me to dream so. Viren today, all of 51, balding, a bit paunchy, and tending towards a double chin. Only his nose and brow remain unchanged. Against the evening light – he does invoke a certain romance. And he still blows smoke rings. Only now, he blows them as he sits with legs crossed, leaning back against his wrought iron chair in his green-edged terrace flat off Peddar Road, and his eyes don't watch the birds any more. I still watch him though – and I can see he is in a world as far away from mine, as he has always been. But I can see the idealist is gone – the Uncle Viren who spoke of socialism and a world where there would be no poor and no rich but a society of equals, the Uncle Viren who spoke of being the one to change the world one day, is dead. And he did not die of T.B. and not of pining for me. Success killed him. Success – not defeat.

I wonder, as I wander sad and palely loitering through our posh flat, with its granite floors and its period furniture and chandelier fittings, if Deepa had left Viren because she knew what he really had become. I wonder, as my feet sink into the thick pile of carpeting in the sunken living room, if Deepa would have done better to have stayed. She could have changed things, perhaps. Stopped the rot. Or maybe she couldn't. And knew it. And so, she left.

Deepa was my enemy. I hated her the day my mother

told me on my return from school, one day in Patna, that Uncle Viren was getting married. She showed me a picture. Deepa, she said. She will be his wife. The picture stared at me, with large, doleful eyes, from under a smooth, white forehead dotted by a tiny *bindi*. The lips smiled softly. I scowled back. My eyes filled. I turned swiftly and walked out of the room till my mother could see me no more – then ran all the way to my favourite corner under the garden tree, and cried and cried my hate deep into my heart.

I hated Deepa silently as I sat watching her dressed in red, sitting proudly with bent head while the priests incanted and chanted and pronounced her Viren's wife. Uncle Viren married Deepa in summer, and mother chose to visit her brother and attend the wedding. In her own way, mother quite fancied Uncle Viren. She had a softer corner for romantic faces too, I think, though she'd never admit it.

Uncle Viren blew smoke rings into my face, when I scowled at him, as he and Deepa came up to me, as man and wife for the first time. He laughed and threw an arm around my shoulders, and held me to his side. My little princess is jealous, he said, and nudged me. I bit my lip and found anger choking my throat. I swore never to see Viren again.

Dreams. My life is full of them. Viren crossed my life in many ways. I finished college and took up a job. Much against mother's wish, I was assigned a Bombay posting. Daddy retired and took off with mother to Madurai. I found myself a flat as a paying guest; and started a slow but steady climb up the social and career ladder. I couldn't stay still for more than a little while at a time – remember?

It was at a party thrown by my boss that I met Viren

again. No, I had not forgotten him. Nor forgiven him. I hated him. Forever. And to prove my hate, I had a proper merry-go-round of boyfriends. At work, outside my work circle. On trips to Madurai. Men found me attractive, and I found I could forget my anger when I was with them. And when I loved them, they helped me forget Viren. And when I left them, I could imagine I was leaving Viren. Leaving him to languish. Die of T.B., for me. Alone. On the terrace.

Everything fell into place when I saw Viren again. He looked much the same at first glance. I caught sight of his profile and the smoke rings – and the breath caught in my throat. I found myself moving, slowly, slowly towards him. Unsure. Was it he?

I bumped into a low table, spilling half a dozen glasses of the best scotch whisky. And Viren turned at the noise. His eyes caught mine, and my heart fell. I knew, I had lived a farce all those years. I had never forgiven myself. I had never forgotten Viren.

He was definitely older. He should be 35-37 now, greying. A touch of dark under his eyes, crows' feet around the corners. A hint of grey at the 7 o'clock shadow on the chin. But still dapper, smart. Everything so right. As if a designer had put him together for a shoot. Like his smoke rings. Perfectly formed. He came up to me – and I could feel his hands on my arms – through the silk of my sleeves. Warm hands holding my arms tight. "Meenu – is it you? How beautiful you have become. What a surprise."

I held the touch of those fingers on my arms through the night. I held too the memory of the look in Deepa's eyes. Of hurt? Of emptiness? Or indecision? I don't know what it was, but the look haunted me, though I had seen it only for a moment. Not a second more. Then she had smiled, her eyes had flashed with warmth, and she was hugging me, holding my hands in hers, saying "Meenu – how are you? I haven't seen you for years. I often wonder about you."

Wonder about me – she hardly knew me. But we soon mended that. Maybe the look, the momentary look I had seen, mesmerised me, maybe I was lonely and warmed to the warmth of her friendship, or maybe I was using these excuses to be near Viren again. But I started visiting Deepa and Viren quite regularly. And Deepa became a friend. I could never be a friend to the wife of the only man I had ever loved.

I could have spent the rest of my life being a friend. Spending evenings watching Viren blow smoke rings, as Deepa and I chatted or played scrabble. Often he'd come in late, after an official party. Often he'd be on tour. He was pretty high up in the ranks now – and quite a man of power. I surmised that. And sometimes wondered at the change in him. No more socialism. No more dreams. He was headed resolutely for the top – and that was all that mattered. We teased him about it, Deepa and I – in our effort to rekindle the old Viren I had known – but he would get up and walk away, and lock himself out beyond the glass doors, on his green-edged terrace. And sit blowing smoke rings. I'd ache for him, and watch Deepa's eyes get the momentary strange, vacant look again – then we'd pretend nothing was wrong, and talk of what to cook. I became Viren's mistress, in spite of Deepa. I pitied her, and empathised with her – for her marriage was a sham. Maybe because they had no children – maybe because he had grown away from her dreams, from being the man she had married – they had nothing in common. He could not even get angry with her. He'd just walk away.

I could not walk away from the fascination the marriage had for me. I watched them destroy it slowly and steadily; and built my own life on the ruins. The day Viren got a promotion, and insisted on getting drunk at the club — and had a fight, which made Deepa lock herself in her bedroom — that was the day I found myself finally in Viren's arms. Too late — after too many years of waiting. But he was a part of my being — and there was no logic, no reasoning that could stop me. I became his mistress.

And when Deepa moved out of the house one day — quietly, without a fuss, just packing her bags and leaving a note to say she wouldn't be back for long and Viren should not come seeking her — I moved in.

No, Deepa did not leave because of me. She knew nothing about our relationship — Viren's and mine. I was careful, discreet. I had years of scheming and loving and dreaming behind me to know how to play the game so that no card was revealed. Viren, on his part, kept his end up too. Not a look would pass between us when Deepa was around. No gesture, no movement, nothing of the reserves of passion that would explode when we were alone.

Deepa's leaving left me bereft of a friend. But I gained a lover, and a status. And the pile carpet in the living room was so much nicer than the rug in my landlady's flat. As was the Queen Anne furniture and the chandelier lighting fixtures.

The world around us accepted. Even my parents accepted. Especially when the divorce came through — and Viren was free to marry me.

It was two days before my marriage that I saw the real Viren. The Viren who would never be still, who would stop at nothing. But it was too late, and the warning went unheeded. I spent the next week in a haze of celebratory champagne.

Today, as I sit on the terrace watching Viren blowing smoke rings into the still humid evening air, I remember those evenings at Madurai. They seem as distant as those people below us seem from 23 floors up. Viren does not speak. And I cannot be still. I talk and joke, and prattle on — to keep my mind from thinking. I repeat my old jokes, recreate childish banter to try and bring back the Viren I knew. The idealist who could change the world. I try at night not to lie awake and think of the things, as a wife. Things I may never have known as a mistress. The deals, the tradeoffs, the hands reddened with the blood spilt by others. Viren's political ambitions have fuelled my nightmares — I can see a long road full of milestones, each milestone a gaping, bloodied skull.

Besides me, in the twin bed, a hand's breath away, Viren snores lightly and turns often. I watch him smiling in his sleep — I imagine he dreams of power and success, of babies beyond imagination — of cash and kind, of bridging the gap from bureaucrat to power monger. A fast closing gap.

I walk the house through the night, trying to widen the gap. But it is too late. So I spend the evenings we are at home — rare evenings those — chattering, fluttering about, talking, talking. I can't be still for a moment.

Sometimes I can see Viren watching me, a strange question in his eyes. But mostly he watches the sky as he smokes. There are no birds here, on the Bombay skyline. No breeze makes the trees curve gracefully across. So he watches, vacant. Sometimes I serve him a drink, and down two myself. Sometimes, I watch the sky too. Sometimes, for old time's sake, I lean over the balcony and pretend to watch the traffic. I hope, at such times, I will fool him into thinking I will lean too far, and force him to get up quickly and rush to hold me back.

But he never does seem to notice how far I lean. He never does get up to hold me back. His eyes are lost in his dreams. As for me – the dreams seem easier and easier. All I need to do is to lean – lean – lean a bit too far. And I will be free. Flying out like a bird.

Maybe Viren will stop midway through blowing smoke rings, when he sees me flying past, above his head, into the far horizon.

12

LAST SUPPER

FOUR STEPS UP. Turn right from the lift. Three floors. Turn right again. I could do it blindfolded. I ring the bell and as it sets up its ridiculously cheerful pealing behind the door, I imagine the hot, fragrant meal, the baby asleep, tiny fists curled against its cheek...

The meal you didn't cook. The baby you wouldn't have—you open the door and I step into reality. Reality is a beautiful home; coir floor, cushions with mirror work, ethnically perfect curtains, plants, glass bric-a-brac carefully collected, perfectly placed. Reality is all this—and us. Two beautiful people, permanently flawed.

Your rocking chair is empty – no book lying face down on the side table either. I have changed into a fresh shirt; the last clean one of the lot. Normally, I'd keep it for tomorrow; but tomorrow can wait. Today's the big day, the big night. I can't meet it unprepared. A year ago, I'd have crossed the black and white rug across the living room and walked whistling into your room, demanding instant attention. But I am wiser now, and though the door is open, I wait for you to come out.

When you do come out, it is from the kitchen with a

LAST SUPPER

tray of tea and biscuits. "Where's Nita?" I ask. "Why did you bother?" how formal I sound even to myself. Your smile throws surprise at me. "I've given her the evening off," you say, handing over the cup. Questions jostle, tumbling to fall into speech, but I hold them in. you don't like questions, I know – and I don't want to spoil tonight.

You offer me a biscuit, and even as the tension mounts while I chew it, and wonder whether I should ask you out for dinner, you throw the next one at me. "Enjoy your tea," you say, "I've to finish the cooking..."

I help you lay the table. You are precise in the way you go about it – yet so elaborate. I notice you have spread your lace and damask tablecloth, the one your *maushi* made for our wedding; and taken out the bone china plates. I am touched, but my mind notes it is your way of adding the touch of finality to the evening. You might as well have written 'Last Supper' on the tablemats!

Over dinner, you are the perfect hostess. Your smile is real, your skin glows with an unspoken excitement. Even the sari you are wearing is beautiful – new perhaps. The food is excellent. My plate, you make sure, is constantly filled. I eat studiously, cursing myself for not buying you some flowers while coming home.

I make your kind of conversation – how the day was, who said what, whether I will clinch the deal – but my mind holds onto the picture, in the bedroom. Of my suitcase waiting lined up alongside the bed; of the clothes lying strewn all over, clothes that I must fold and pack before I leave.

I know what it's going to be like. You'll glitter and dazzle and smile, as you say goodbye – still playing the perfect hostess; and I, feeling a guest already in my own house – this house which is no longer my home – will leave without saying any of the obvious things. Maybe it will be better this way, maybe I'll be spared from the clichés of such a situation.

But surely, I tell myself, as I look quickly down at my plate, to hide my eyes, you cannot really be so unfeeling. Somewhere it must be getting to you, as it is getting to me. You, who cry unabashedly at movies, who can't see a puppy yelping without going soft-eyed yourself – even I could not have turned your heart completely.

I look up, to meet your silent gaze. Questioning. The guard is dropped "Nina," I begin, "is it finally goodbye, then?" You smile a smile that is neither no, nor yes. It's a smile that transforms me; I can see the old Nina somewhere in it. Independent yet clinging, self-willed yet trusting, willing to be led. Was it I who failed, by not leading or was it that you disapproved of the direction I was going in? I reach forward to touch your hand, to capture the mood and knock over my glass of water – but I might as well have spilt the salt. You withdraw into yourself, busy putting me at ease, wiping the table dry.

Years ago, a guest had spilt a drop of gravy on this same tablecloth. You had fussed exactly like this, rushing about blotting the stain, and assuring him it was of no import – but you were seething inside. The last goodbye had hardly been said, and I had hardly closed the door and turned back but you had already swiped the tablecloth off the table and rushed away with it to the bedroom. When I followed you asking if I could help, you turned on me, eyes full of angry tears. "How dare you?" you had said. "How dare you tell Nita to lay this tablecloth for your uncouth friends?" We had made up after that quarrel – but tonight there is no making up. My awkward movement has sent us back in time, touching each irreparable breach on the way, and we are back to where we were when the meal began. Absolute strangers.

You've cleared away the dishes; and changed the music. I can smell the souffle before it comes and my heart turns. I remember the time you joked about our child being chocolate-skinned – because both of us loved chocolates and ate so much of it. Perhaps if we had had a child–but that was another goof-up. When you were willing, I wasn't prepared. Not ready for parenthood, uncertain of my future, I forced you to wait. And then, when I began to feel the generation passing, seeing my best years rolling past, you had your music, and your recitals. All those fences you built to keep me away – to fence yourself in, for I did not know then that you were fencing yourself from loneliness – from acknowledging that we were temperamentally mismatched; you a doer, an achiever, who wanted me to climb; I, a dreamer, willing to throw up my job to write a book, travel in strange places, or even tend a baby. Well – I never did throw up my job – but you didn't have the baby either. All we had was his name – Arvind – and even that is not really ours, since you borrowed it from your dead brother.

"The soufflé is delicious," I exclaim. "Please have some more," you say. I pat my middle. "I'm stuffed," I say. You would have said, "Silly," in the past and giggled; and now... you giggle and say, "Silly," then move off to clear the plates.

The music comes to a rasping close. It is like a cue. A silence has descended on us. On you. It is as if your role has run out; but the curtain won't come down. And you don't know what to do. I don't either. I look at you, at my hands. At my feet. Remember then, that my black shoes are still at the cobbler's since yesterday.

I mumble something about a nice evening and enter the bedroom. I am half hoping you will follow, will stop me with a line, some inane, meaningless line that will mean, don't go yet, but you have settled down on the rocking chair. And in the rock-rock of wood against the floor, I feel the seconds running out.

I push the jumble of clothes into the suitcase. Then remember it's the Delsey I bought you on my last trip abroad. Oh well, I can always return it later.

I must look ridiculous carrying the suitcase and the bags all at once. But you don't laugh. Don't even smile. Only your face glows with suppressed, unspoken excitement.

I place the bags outside the door – then come back to say goodbye. You permit me to take your hand; you look me in the eyes. "Thank you for everything," you say – I don't know whether you're thanking me for leaving you the house and all your things in it, or for just leaving.

As I turn away, you reach out and kiss my cheek.

Three floors down, four steps down, turn left. As I open the car door, I remember, I've done it again – left my toothbrush hanging in the bathroom.

13

A TOOTHFUL TALE

RAMA BHUA WOULD not have lost her dentures if only she had listened to me and kept them in her mouth. But when had Rama Bhua ever listened to anybody?

Ever since she knew she had to go Moradabad to attend Kiron's wedding, Rama Bhua had scaled that height of excitement that put her above reason. "I don't care what she does, I give up," Mukund Phuphaji had grumbled after a vocal battle with her, and he had lifted his office bag and disappeared. He kept to his word and did not discuss the trip to Moradabad after that. But somehow it was understood that he was not coming along, and that I would have the honour instead of escorting Bhuaji to the wedding and back. For all Phuphaji cared, he said, Rama could come and go as she pleased; he had washed his hands off her. I could not do the same now, and thus bore the brunt of her demands and excitement. Not that I grudged doing so, for, after all, if it were not for Bhuaji's ready hospitality, I would be languishing in a hostel, and I, for one, have never liked hostel life.

There was still a month to go for the wedding when Daya Tauji wrote inviting us for it and it did not matter either, that we were to make the trip only a week before the event. As far as Rama Bhua was concerned, she was already on her way to the station, and if she did not hurry, the train would leave without her.

"I must take my jewels, and enough food, and 300 rupees for the wedding gift; and a gold ring for the *mu dikhai* ceremony," she repeated, each time she saw me or Phuphaji. I kept a discreet silence. Phuphaji made a grumpy face and gave her the money. Then there was silence in the house while Rama Bhua sat at the jewellers, getting a ring made for Kiron's bride, seeing to it personally that the gold was not half copper and the pearls were not plastic.

"Beti, we must get my jewels today. I must look through them and decide which I can take with me," she announced. So I went along with her, and patiently listened to the account of Kiron's childhood days, and the trouble his parents had gone through to get him a wife of his choice, which she narrated for the general information of the rickshawman and any passers-by who might be interested.

"Bhuaji," I said, when we were safely inside the bank. "Don't you think it is unsafe to talk about our trip? Someone might try to rob us of the jewels."

"I know that, beti," Rama Bhua said condescendingly, with a knowing smile. "Whether you tell them or not, people who want to know about these things, know anyway. But let them think me a fool. I will fool them instead; they will never get my jewels." And she smiled again, very knowingly indeed.

When the day of the journey dawned, Rama Bhua was all prepared to meet it. "Wake up, beti," she grumbled, "we have to set our for Moradabad today, or have you forgotten?"

As if I could forget. Bhuaji's conversation for the past week had been only about what to eat on the journey, what to carry, how to pack, which saris I should take, and what she should and should not do at Moradabad. And the whole of last night, her hurried movements had disturbed my sleep as she moved suitcases and opened and shut *almirah* doors in a flurry of packing.

I had a hectic week ahead of me, if her plans were any indication, for it would be my unenviable duty to go with her to the homes of her various relatives in Moradabad, after the wedding was over, for Bhuaji thought it good training for a girl of marriageable age to learn family protocol first hand. Also, considering that Moradabad is something of a stronghold of Bhuaji's in-laws, the visits were unavoidable. I consoled myself with the thought that there would be a lot of good eating included.

The train was at 4 p.m. Phuphaji refused to make a trip from the office to see us off. "Spare me," he had murmured, when Bhuaji had asked him whether he would be coming home, or to the station, and that was that.

At 3 o'clock, the servant boy was dispatched to hail a taxi, "It wouldn't do for us to miss the train, Daya will come to meet us at Moradabad and will be disappointed," Bhuaji said when I told her that there was ample time yet.

It was lucky the cab came when it did, for we just made it on time. It took a full 15 minutes to load the luggage. There was a huge holdall that Bhuaji and I had tied down with rope; for Moradabad, Bhuaji said, would be very cold in February, and she had to carry her *razai*. There was my small suitcase, and her large one. These, I knew about, too. What I did not know about was the kerosene tin, and the water *ghara* and the large pink plastic bag that Bhuaji emerged from the kitchen with, as the cab man was shutting the door of the boot. "These are eats for the journey," she announced, pointing to the kerosene tin, even before I could ask her about it. "And this holds my jewels," she said, her voice loud enough to make the cab driver shift the expression on his face to one of alert interest. She thrust the plastic bag under my nose, and I caught a glimpse of packets wrapped in newspaper. Honestly, Rama Bhua could be naïve, I told myself, and decided that the only way to avoid featuring in such situations in future was to shift to a hostel, on my return. If I returned, that is, and did not lose my life protecting her ill-concealed jewels.

The moment we were settled into the train, crushed between the kerosene tin and the *ghara*, Bhuaji decided to make a trip to the bathroom. She returned looking older by ten years. It was only when she opened her mouth that I realised she was minus her teeth. "I have put them in the plastic bag, along with the soap and *paan supari* dish, to make the packet look heavier," she said in a low voice, her toothless mouth blowing hot air into my embarrassed ear. "The jewels are in my trunk, but everyone will think they are with me and they won't bother about the trunk." Her pink gums shone with delight over her ingenuity.

I was moved to praise; though I did think this fuss was unnecessary. And I still did not understand why the dentures had to go into the bag.

"Beti, you are really dense," Bhuaji hissed, "Can't you see? If I look old and toothless, and hug the bag close, people will think I am really a senile old lady who will be foolish enough to carry her jewels in her hand…"

Bhuaji spent that night sleeping peacefully, holding her plastic bag tight. I spent another sleepless night, sandwiched between the suitcase with the jewels and the kerosene tin. And when Moradabad approached, the jewels were still as safe as they had been. No one had even looked at the trunk, though quite a few eyes had lingered over the plastic bag, which seemed pinker and larger than ever.

As Moradabad station drew close, Bhuaji disappeared again into the bathroom to wash her face and comb her hair and put on the armour necessary for better talk and broader smiles.

Five minutes later, her scream rent the air. I leapt to the bathroom door and knocked on it, imagining thieves closeted in with Bhuaji, grabbing at her plastic bag. Bhuaji opened the door and cried toothless into my shoulder. It took all of ten minutes to get the story out, and, by that time, Daya Tauji was there to hear it too.

Bhuaji had washed her face and powdered it, and painted a large *bindi* on her forehead. She was almost on her way out when she had smiled into the mirror appreciatively and discovered her toothless state. She fumbled in the bag and drew out the dentures. And as the train jerked to a halt, she cracked her head against the wash basin, and the dentures had slipped out, and fallen....right into the open flush pan...

I told her I had been right when I felt the dentures should have remained in her mouth. She did not argue with me. It was the quietest fortnight I had with Rama Bhua... who did not dare to display her dentureless gums at the wedding.

14

A SUNDAY EVENING

I AM PRETENDING to read, but I am watching you. Covertly. As if I have never seen you before. Sometimes I feel I haven't; some movement you make is so new, so different from all the others I've seen before, that I feel you are someone new. Not quite known.

That flick of the wrist, for example – it got me, just now. The way you brushed the back of your hand across your forehead, pushing back that stray lock – I have never seen you do that before. The gesture wrenched at me. I had seen her doing it a hundred times, loved the way she flicked her wrist at the end of the movement. Such finality. As if to say, "There you go, your lock of hair – don't come back." We used to laugh about it; her sweep-off gesture, we called it. And now you. You must have picked it up from her, if she still has it. Or maybe gestures are hereditary too. And she has passed them on just as she gave you her eyes, her fine, silky hair, her long lashes, and her temper.

You look up suddenly, your eyes wide, questioning. What is it *Appa?* You want to know. I smile. Nothing son, I say, I was looking at your drawing. What is that? Superman, you say, and bring it closer, thrusting the sheet so close to

A SUNDAY EVENING

my face I can smell the colours. Yes, yes, Superman, I say, looking at it from a more reasonable distance. If I look long enough, my paternal pride can even discern a flying cape in the mass of squiggles you have made.

You go back to your drawing. I watch you, afraid. Soon it will be night; and dinner time. Then time to sleep. And before I can finish my dream, our day together will be gone. Monday morning, and your other world, the sane sensible world of school books and homework, violin lessons and home-cooked meals will claim you. I, of course, will go back to being the workaholic I am known to be. Computers are a bit like people, and I can forget everything, everyone, while with them. Almost. Everyone, except you. Everything, except the fact that you are no longer mine. As if anyone can deny our relationship.

It is a strange thing, this, our relationship. You are not quite son; I am not quite father. Fathers scold, pet, teach; I do none of these. Sons giggle, cry, learn. You do some of these. Once a month is not enough to get me into the role of father. You, of course, have more practice at being a son – your mother's son – but a son all the same; so you are better at your role than I am. But you are a clever child; something of a changeling. You adapt to my ineptitude; and abandon your role to suit mine. As a result, quite often, we are friends. Just friends. Good friends. One would think we were inseparable, seeing us at such times. No one would guess ours is a transitory relationship. Fleeting as only a Sunday can be; especially when it comes only once in a month.

You are hungry. I can see it in the way you have begun to chew on your lip. That strange restlessness, that begins from within and takes you over, comes from hunger. You do not know it. You only find Superman not quite so absorbing; your impatience with him makes you scratch your colouring pen all across the page.

I pick you up then, and say brightly – Where shall we go to eat today? To Kamats? Or Delhi Durbar? Or Open House? The names fill my stomach with the dread knowledge that the day is moving irrevocably to its end. Before long, my picnic will be over.

Snowman's, you say, eyes alight. You can't have ice cream for dinner, you had it for lunch, I say. But I had a sandwich too, at 4 o'clock, you say – and I can see her look come into your eyes, as I begin to remonstrate. Snowman. *Appa*, Snowman – your wrists beat a light tattoo on my shoulders; light, too light – you have lost your baby fat long before your babyhood.

At Snowman's, I am watching you again. You order an ice cream so big that you have to stand up to look down into the glass; and when you look up, there's jelly on the tip of your nose. You laugh and make faces at yourself as I show you your face in the mirror. I smile, but cannot laugh. On such Sundays, I cannot laugh after noon. The hours that are left gnaw into me, devouring whatever laughter I'm capable of.

Three ice creams later, you are ready to leave. You want to rush home, to watch that last movie on the video. Your video watching is as strictly rationed as my chances of watching you grow, and like me, you want to make the most of it.

Mickey Mouse is as silly as he was when I was a child – and I can see myself now, in the way you stuff your knuckles into your mouth as you giggle. In the photograph that used to stand by our bedside, the one taken long before you were born, I am laughing just like that, and she is looking at me from your wide, wondering eyes.

A SUNDAY EVENING

I wish I knew how to talk to you – but 34 years make a bad bridge for conversation between us. I should have learnt to talk with you, when you were around all the time, but I was too busy then making my career, finding my executive level, listening to computers talking – to find time to listen to you. And then, when you went away, I suddenly had so much to tell you. Even now the words are straining at my throat, pushing against my chest – but I do not know how to say them to you. How does one tell a six-year-old son all he wants to say? Maybe, as the Sundays go past, you will hear what I say without my saying it – and understand.

Your eyes cloud with sleep. Your laughter dulls. Mickey Mouse goes the way Superman did – down the abyss of your restlessness. I know better than to take you to bed, though. I move closer and let you snuggle against the crook of my arm. And as your head grows heavy against me, I know it is time.

You sleep curled up, dormouse like, against my side. I lie awake, watching you smile at some childish dream. I cannot sleep. On other nights, when I am too restless to sleep, I switch on the Amiga 2000 and plot programmes on it till my mind grows numb and heavy. Tonight, I prefer to listen to your breathing, to feel the rise and fall of your tiny chest against my ribs. Tonight, as since 9 a.m. today, I am Parent, Protector, Father. Forever. Till Monday do us part.

15
AFTER THE BOMB

IN THE DESOLATE wastes, nothing stirred... Nothing broke the eye's route as it travelled from one horizon to the other – searching. Only the earth – parched, broken, taut – spent badland that would never sustain life. Never again.

Eons ago – life had thrived here. In this dreary expanse – earth's most desolate wastes – human life had never dared to set foot. Yet nature had peopled it with her own denizens – creatures that crawled and breathed, lived within the crevices that fissured the desert land, vying for the infrequent moisture that dampened the area with the spiny vegetation that dotted the low-lying troughs. Nature watched in silence as battles were waged between creatures that crawled over the desert wastes and the hardier, immobile plants. Often in years of severe drought – when even the stray cloud did not drop its wet into the soil – the crawlies would feed on the plants, stripping them of their scanty flesh till only a heap of spiky plant bones remained. Yet, at the first hint of damp, the spikes would reappear – making eerie patterns on the ground, battling silently for the scanty nutrition with the crawlies. Year after year. Nothing changed. Sometimes, the crawlies died in great numbers – sometimes the plants were wiped out – but both reappeared to remain, at most times, constant in number.

That was before the bomb. Without warning, one day the bomb ended the quiet, well-planned battle that nature had set up for her recreation. The badlands exploded – a cloud rose from the ground, a cloud thicker, denser, heavier than any the region had ever seen. It filled the earth with poison, and as it lifted slowly into the sky – the very air died a quick, permanent death. For days, weeks, eons, the cloud stood shadowing the desert land – and, under its vigil, no creature dared to stir. When it fragmented and dissolved, nothing remained, Nothing. Not a crawly – not a burnt twig, not a brown spiky thorn. The badland had ousted nature.

Yet this day – this day that was like any other – dark, despairing, desolate, something stirred. An eye opened, then shut as the light blinded it. Then, cautiously it opened, again. It surveyed the surroundings. Nothing, Only cracked, grey earth, with a cover of fine dust over it and the grey sky. Nothing else.

A sound. The eye had a ear – or how could it hear? The head, there was one – turned, the eye looked – into another eye. The creature was not alone. From a rock nearby – a second eye stared back. Unblinking. Cold.

By noon, the sun created waves out of the dust, it shimmered and shone, and rippled, though not a breeze stirred in the wastes. The new inhabitants of the badlands looked up at the sun. Three large eyes, each on an oval head, staring unblinking, unfazed at the punishing sun.

Somewhere in the eons between the bomb and now, the stage had been set for their birth. The crawlies had died long ago. Nothing in the wasteland was prepared for this. Yet it happened. After years of lying dead under the surface, three crawly eggs had stirred with life. Deep in the fissure of a crack which chance had shielded from the heat, a process had started – continued – and ended at a speed a hundred times slower than normal. The eggs had lain dormant but not dead. Like the undead rising from their graves, the embryos stirred, congealed into more coherent forms of life – and finally as they tired of waiting, began to break out. It was a long process, a tiring one – the once fragile shells had turned rock-hard with time. Yet nature had compensated. The claws, each a pointed chisel, hammered and scratched and finally fragmented the barrier – and the crawlies emerged, staring popeyed into the unwelcoming outside.

Nothing stared back at the three eyes, except the unrelenting sun. But the crawlies were not troubled. They had survived the great scorching heat and power of the bomb – they would survive the desert sun. Effortlessly.

Twenty-five years later

A morning like any other. The desert badlands lie wrapped in grey. Grey dust below, grey sky above. Something stirs. An aircraft cuts into the thick air, slows, hovers – then lands shakily. The dust flies in grey clouds from the wind of its rotating wings. Behind the exhaust, the grey dust forms an elongated tail, making the craft resemble a giant, thrashing insect. Nothing else stirs. Only hidden in the dark crevices, a thousand eyes watch.

Dr. Venkatraman and Dr. Roy Chowdhary are the first men to enter the badland in years. Finding it inhospitable, they decide not to opt for the tent they had hopefully brought along, but to conduct their investigations from within the craft. The craft is well-equipped for living in – the temperature inside is in marked contrast to the 75° C + outside; and the cool, green, plush furnishing of the living area is an invitation to comfort. But the two men are not there to rest. They enter the living area only to sleep – an exhausted, dreamless sleep that demands complete surrender. Most of the time they are in the front of the craft – in the lab, where they watch, and discuss and record their findings. Day after day.

From the diary of Roy Chowdhary

The badlands have fascinated many but few have dared venture into them. Before the bomb, government planes flew over the area to make sure there was no life in the region. As no human life of even a nomadic nature was spotted, the helicopters never touched ground. The region was declared suitable for the bomb test because it was not only devoid of human life, but also of animal and plant life.

Any vegetation that existed was of the lowest order. Dispensable.

The bomb was 75 years ago. After the test, the place acquired a character of a challenge for the adventurous. But the government had declared it a dangerous prohibited place, and none of the daredevils who wanted to trek, ride or drive across into the badlands got a chance to indulge their death wish. Scientists ignored it – after the mishap that overtook the three-member team that went into the region soon after the area was declared 'reasonably safe' after the bomb. The team had maintained contact with the head office 150 kms away, then mysteriously disappeared. Air sorties sent to search for them found no trace of the aircraft or the bodies.

We are here, of course, as a freelancer team. Dr. Venkatraman is a geologist and I am a biologist – we sneaked into the area this morning. It was quite easy. The entire arrangement took a week or so, after our meeting at a science seminar, where we discovered our common preoccupation with the forbidden land.

Entering the area was easier than we had thought possible. Once we had the craft, we sailed in, hovering at above eye level at the check post – then coming lower to just above the rugged surface. We travelled for a few hours thus, till we were well into the desert, before deciding to land.

The excitement has been too much – I am exhausted just writing this, and Venkatraman is cooking a meal for us. He says he's ravenous. We rested and waited till evening before we decided to venture out.

At dusk, we set up our observation posts. Venkatraman was sure we would find the exotica by way of minerals and rocks thrown up or even created by the bomb's force. I am not so hopeful; there seems no sign of life whatsoever. What am I supposed to investigate? Venkatraman is determined to go out. I have dissuaded him. Even at dusk, the heat is intense – our craft's thermometer records $60°$ C at 5 p.m.

I must mention the look of the area at dusk. As evening fell, the grey deepened gradually, till it turned a rich purple. The sky looked as if an aluminium lid had been put over the earth. We could not feel the heat inside the craft, of course, but outside, the very colouring was suffocating. The clouds were oppressive, hanging so low you could almost stretch out and touch them – and what fantastic shapes. I am not sure whether the clouds are moving down or upwards from the heated earth – a few kilometres away, some of them seemed to touch the ground.

At night, it was so quiet – deathly quiet. Our craft-ear recorded no sound. I had hoped for some hiss perhaps, a creak or a crack – some resilient voice that mocked the deathliness of the place – but not even the air breathed. There were no trees, of course, so, even if there had been a wind, there would have been no welcoming brush of leaves against the microphones.

Venkatraman noticed the phenomenon first. He had been staring intently at the screens for a long time while I thought he had fallen asleep with his eyes open. I have a cousin who does that – and Venkatraman has the same kind of hooded eyes. But, suddenly, he jumped up, and rushed to the top of the hatch, where the groundoscope was latched. There is an element of risk in using the groundoscope; to lower it, one must open a section of the hatch and push the end through, and, at that moment, outside air would enter the craft. But Venkatraman was too excited to think of the risk. He quickly uncovered the groundoscope and fixed his eyes greedily to the glass.

My excitement mounted proportionately, as I watched him swivel the groundoscope around, peering at now this part of the ground – now that. After a century of suspense, he beckoned to me.

"Look, can you make out what that is – I give up," he said, as I peered through the glass.

At first, they looked like unblinking glow-worms – glistening quietly in the rubble, shining through the dust. But I knew they were not glow-worms. They formed a patch, odd shaped, almost a diamond – at a 45-degree angle from the craft. Nowhere else could the groundoscope spot a similar patch. It was, I decided, some strange metal, in tiny mica-like particles, embedded in the ground. "Then why the strange shape?" Venkatraman asked, when I gave him my faltering opinion.

We debated over the mystery for a while. If only we could get closer – then Venkatraman struck his head with his palm. "Fool!" he said, to me as much as to himself. "Of course, we can get closer!" and he moved to the controls of the craft. I marvelled at the speed with which he could move his bulk when he wanted to – at most other times, he just sits bunched up in chair like a giant toad!

He moved the craft 45 degrees to the south – a few metres closer to the patch. Now the grandoscope would be almost directly above the shining mass. But his jubilant 'Aah!' as he returned to the instrument turned into a cry of utter surprise. There was nothing below the groundoscope – he could see only dusty, grey rubble. I stared too, uncomprehendingly, then gasped as I moved the groundoscope higher. There, at exactly the same distance from the craft, at the same angle, the mass shone dull. Only this time, it was not such an organised shape – and seemed somewhat smaller. Venkatraman went mad at his own incomprehension of the phenomenon. But here was something at last. He would have stepped out then – that very moment – but I stopped him. If it was just rubble – it would wait. If it wasn't and chances were it wasn't – for how could rubble move? – then it would be wiser for us to wait till morning.

We spent a sleepless night, of course – and, at the first hint of the dull, grey-hued dawn, made preparations to step out.

We decided to take turns exploring the outside. Any fear in us had been nullified completely by the excitement of a possible discovery. Venkatraman would go first – it was, he claimed, his right. After all, it was his discovery!

He left at 6 a.m. sharp. The cooler suit made him look like a spaceman about to burst – but it would protect him from the heat, and from whatever else waited in that desolate air to assault him. He was to stay out for exactly 30 minutes – I had to tug the end of the rope that anchored him to our craft to remind him that the time was up, and he had then to replace his cooler suit. Very unfortunate we could not get one of the more modern versions that can work for half a day – but even this had been difficult enough.

He stepped out with his lenses and a little pickaxe, a shovel and a tiny box for samples. I watched him plodding around, looking like the man on the moon and worried whether he would bring back any perils after his contact with the outside. But the air had come in last night and in plenty while he climbed out of the hatch – and no damage had been caused. So I told myself not to be an alarmist.

Venkatraman heaved himself back into the craft, jingling like a coin box when the pickaxe and shovel touched the metal side of the craft. I had called thrice before he would come in – and he had turned red as a brick under his suit, which had begun to turn warm. The thermometer recorded 68° C, and three per cent humidity.

We examined the scraping of the soil that he had brought along. All morning, we picked and shifted and analysed – but nothing extraordinary revealed itself. There was dust; bomb dust, thick and heavy like sifted lava – and soil, and rocks of many kinds – but nothing to explain the gleaming shine that we had seen at night.

The only way to get to the bottom of the mystery was to go out and examine the gleaming at night.

Venkatraman decided he would go out again.

Tonight.

That night, we looked through the groundoscope and there it was. Tantalisingly out of reach, glistening and gleaming like stars in the dust. Unmoving, unique. Venkatraman could not restrain himself. He climbed out as quickly as he could – ignoring the safety line – insisting he would be back long before the half hour. "I'll just walk out, grab a shovelful, and come back," he insisted. I relented in the face of such enthusiasm. And, any way, the thermometer recorded 53° C – which was a very hot night – but one bearable by Indian standards at least!

I watched him plod heavily up to the place where the gleaming soil was – we had decided not to move the craft as it did not help us get any closer. Then his form filled the screen – and I could only see his retreating back.

When he walked back, he was still in the direct line of vision through the screen and his look of triumph was a pleasure to behold. He had taken off the helmet of his cooler suit and waved it triumphantly at me.

Inside, he ripped off his suit – and set to work. Soon triumph turned to dismay. Nothing. Only dust and soil and rock rubble. Nothing else.

That night, Venkatraman was like a mad man. He almost assaulted me when I told him I should go out and pick the next sample. Then, before I could stop him, he was out again. He would stay out, till whatever it was that had moved away, returned to near the craft – then – he would pounce! Since it had moved the first day, when we had moved the craft nearer it – the thing, whatever it was – moved. But it obviously came back to its original place when it sensed no one near. He'd only have to be faster this time. He had it all solved, but I could not fathom much of the mystery. If it moved, it was alive – and what kind of life could this inhospitable place sustain? And if it wasn't alive – what accounted for the sudden disappearances and appearances? And the changing patterns?

I realised with a start that Venkatraman was not in my view-finder. Where had he gone? The mutt! Even a scientific breakthrough did not justify the kind of risk he was taking. Then, as I swivelled the view-finder around, I spotted him, standing still – at a distance from the craft. Without his cooler suit, he had moved very quickly indeed. I peered into the groundoscope – the glittering lights were there – but only a few – almost home. Venkatraman would have to wait a long while for his breakthrough.

I sat back watching him wait. I must have fallen asleep – this was my third sleepless night and sleeping during the day had not been possible that morning with Venkatraman alternately exulting over his discovery and bemoaning his lack of progress with it. I sat up in panic. Where was that man? – he should have returned by now! It was almost 1 p.m. – ten minutes short of it, to be exact. I had slept for almost four hours.

I peered into the view-finder, turning it around this way and that, then caught sight of Venkatraman. He had stretched himself out on the ground – and, hand tucked babylike under a curved chin, was fast asleep. One look at the groundoscope showed little change in the glimmering mass. It had become scantier, if anything. I debated whether I should venture out and wake the exhausted sleeper – but fear of abandoning the craft was greater than my worry about my fellow scientist. And he looked quite comfortable on that rough terrain. Let him be, if he does not wake by 2 p.m., I shall wake him, I resolved. Time hung heavy – I felt disoriented, suspended between half-sleep and complete awakening. I moved into the kitchen area to open a few tins, made myself a meal of sorts, then rested my head against the table. There were still 30 minutes for my self-appointed deadline. I put my head down again on the table and shut my eyes.

A tiny click-click-clack burrowed itself into my consciousness, nudging me awake. I resisted, then remembering, awoke. Sweat broke over my face, as I chanced to see the clock. It was 3 a.m. well past my deadline. And Venkatraman was still missing.

I knocked over the cup and saucer, spilling remnants of coffee on the craft floor, as I rushed to the view-finder. It was as I had expected, Venkatraman was nowhere to be seen. I unlocked the nuts that bound the finder to a semi-circular range and turned it around full circle. But to no end; there was no sign of him. He had moved well out of range.

The groundoscope held another surprise. It revealed nothing. A hint of a glimmer perhaps — but nothing more.

What was I to do?

I decided to wait. There was nothing else — nothing seemed to have an explanation — it was all maddening, baffling. I fought visions of Venkatraman frying in the post-dawn heat — of him lying gasping on the dust. But he had a compass and surely could not get lost. Besides, he would receive directional signals from the craft, on his wrist band; he could not fail to come back, only, he should not stray so far as to be unable, physically, to return. I wished I had forced him to take the cooler suit along. Damn.

There was nothing to be done. To fight the mounting panic, I decided to tidy up the craft a little. Things had slipped considerably where housekeeping was concerned; and the kitchen area especially resembled a bachelor's den rather than a scientist's kitchenette.

AFTER THE BOMB

First things first, I mused, like a housewife. Let me mop up the coffee. The stains will never go otherwise from the fibre tiles.

I gathered up the mop and moved to the table area. There was nothing. No coffee splashes on the floor, no stain. Not a sign of the streak that had lain brown against the white a few minutes ago. It could not have evaporated – the craft was too cool for that – and the humidity was at a controlled, comfortable 60 per cent. I was more than perplexed. Worried. Here was a new dilemma, to add to the old one! Without thinking, automatically I carried my cup and saucer and plate to the sink. Halfway there, I noticed with a start – the half crust of bread I had put on the plate had vanished.

I looked around the tiny area – no, Venkatraman could not have sneaked in, though practical jokes were up his street. There was no one, nothing in the living room area either. I moved to the intercom television. Then, as I peered closer to the picture, I thought something shone dimly for a twinkling of an eye, then it was gone. I had imagined it – some reflection of light, some optical trick only expected of a sleepless, troubled mind – tripping itself up with worry.

Mechanically now, I moved from room to room – from kitchen area to living room, back to work space. Mechanically, I looked into the viewfinder. Nothing. Where was that man? Fool! Idiot! Irresponsible dullard! I peered into the groundscope. The pattern glistened back at me – dull, but distinct. A definite square.

The clickity click made me turn around. I had heard the sound before. This time, it sounded ominous. I remembered the spilt coffee – and turned suddenly in the direction of the sound – as if to surprise the source.

Nothing. I thought I saw a glimmer.

A careful examination of the desk proved futile. Only a few sheets, a pen, a geiger counter, and an ink bottle. Venkatraman had this quaint fancy for using ink pens. I picked up the geiger counter, wondering if the clicking had emanated from it. The machine was off. I switched it on. It began clicking slowly – each click – the breath of a plastic lung – in-out – click-pause-click-click-pause-click. Something in the place, inside my once-safe haven, was radioactive.

Panic stirred my insides. Venkatraman must have absorbed doses of it. Horrible thought. The air must be heavy with it still. After all these years! Why had we not thought of checking for radiation before we ventured out? There was no question of going out now, the only chance of survival was to scout around for Venkatraman, pick him up, and rush back to safety. What an inglorious end to our adventure of discovery.

I secured the hatch – it stuck initially as if a stone had rolled into the groove – but when I lifted it clear and tried again – it shut smooth and tight. Heaving a sigh of relief, I hastened to the couple of metres off the ground – then I pushed the stick forward and began my search.

I combed the area moving in widening circles for hours till it was dark again, but there was no sign of Venkatraman dead or alive. He had, for all practical purposes, disappeared. Turned into rubble. Another click reminded me of my own exposure to danger – if the air in the craft was indeed radioactive.

It was time for a decision. My mind bent under the weight of the responsibility then sprang back like a diving board after the swimmer has jumped. I felt light-headed – later, perhaps my conscience would bother me and add the weight of remorse to my thoughts – but now! I put the craft into gear and lifted off. Perhaps I would reach land by daybreak. And even summon help. There was no point in staying in the badlands alone. I'd never find Venkatraman that way and probably end up dead too!

As the greyness rushed past me – I relaxed. The nightmare would be over as soon as I got the story off my chest to others. Someone more competent, better armed would take over. Amen. If only the maddening clicking would stop...

In the desert sands, the faint clicking grew in magnitude. The eyes stared unblinking – but where they had once reflected pale and yellow in the moonlight – they shone a deep, fiery red now.

The remains of Venkatraman had been disposed of methodically. First, the swarms had killed him like so many leeches – draining him of his blood to the last drop. A clean operation – not a drop had been spilled and the great body had felt no pain. Then the sharp claws and teeth had shorn off the flesh, mouths gulping it in great hungry gulps to assuage a lifelong hunger. When the swarm had fed, nothing was left, not even a few bones. The entire meal had taken a couple of hours.

Only a few clothes and his mattress remained. The swarm went to work on it – tearing it apart, rolling it in saliva till it formed small, easily transported balls of mush. Then, in a procession, the crawlies marched back to the giant network of nests – to store their bounty. Today, they were fed – their meal would see them through the next generations. Future generations could see the food. Nothing in the lands could be wasted.

As time crawled, replete, the crawlies disappeared

into cracks of the earth – to rest after their huge meal. The great eyes stared unblinking into the sky, their transparent bodies lay in circles, assuming the colour and texture of the surrounding rubble. Then, as night fell, the gentle click clack ceased. Nothing moved in the badlands. Absolutely nothing.

16
RENDEZVOUS

WHEN I REACHED the church compound, the moon had moved across the sky. It hung there, pale and yellow, I could see its wan light through the clouds and through the lattice work the leaves of the silver birch made against the sky.

It was barely past seven, but the winter evening had turned dark, and a chilly wind rose, causing the trees to whisper and rustle.

It was a sound I've loved ever since I could remember, the silver birch trees in the All Saints Church compound whispering in the night, but as I heard the sound, I hurried. I knew she would be afraid. The wind in the trees always made her cry. Once, long ago, a year ago, I had been late on just such a night as this. There had been no moon then; only the light from the blue, illuminated cross over the church spilled weakly on to the garden – and the wind had whispered in the trees.

When I had reached her, a little out of breath with hurrying, a little short-winded due to the beauty of it all and the knowledge that she was there – I had found her crying. She had stood under one of the tall branched trees, dress dark against its silver bark, her body gentle against its slender straightness – head bent into her hands, I had thought she was laughing, but when I touched her face, it was wet with tears – and she clung to me, telling me again and again that she was afraid – the place was full of ghosts from the cemetery at the edge of the garden – she was afraid. I loved her the more for waiting for me then, despite her fear, and promised never to be late again. I made her calm herself down, and listen to the music of the wind in the trees.

She would have had us meet elsewhere, but there was no other place. Nothing as beautiful, as quiet – a perfect setting for our secret meetings twice a week. The rest of the week we were strangers to each other; I was away at a hostel a whole town away – and could visit home only on weekends. And meeting her only twice a week in any less private place was unthinkable.

She would be scared today, I thought, absently buttoning the cuff of my shirt sleeve. Even as I walked the broken stone path that led to our secret garden, and moved towards the wicker gate that separated it from the rest of the walk, the sound of the music from the church swelled. The wind held its breath to listen, the moon bent lower – it was beautiful.

She came running up the broken walk. She wore white, her hair, loose against her face, smelt of honey and mint – freshly washed and dried. I could see her eyes dark against her face – she was not scared. I reached for her, but she held me away – one silken arm held against my chest to warn me. "Wait," she whispered, "I want to show you something."

She tugged at my sleeve, leading me into the tiny garden and beyond it. The little wicker gate swung back on its broken hinge and leaned drunken against the wind — but she had forgotten her love for order — she, who always waited to close it so the ends met just so — let it lurch dizzily in the night, as she hastened on. Compelled by the urgency in her voice, urged by my need to be close — I followed.

We were in the little cemetery — the cold stones rang below my heel — and I knew this was going to be a strange night. An unforgettable one. She, who was afraid of the dark, had led me into the deepest shadows.

The music rose and fell — like an angel breathing pain, the wind whispered in my ears — but I did not heed it. For she was close, the scent of her face brushing mine.

"Did you know her?" she asked and bent quickly to rest on one knee over a grave. "Jennifer, age 22, died 1976," she read, "You must have known her — what was she like?"

My head reeled in astonishment, Jennifer — Jenny! My breath caught the name and held it. Jennifer — I had known Jennifer — so tall, so golden, Jenny, who always smelt of purple flowers. I had, as a boy then, loved her, as she walked the roads of my colony, but she had no eyes for me. I was a child, a freckled school boy, a younger brother's friend. She had smiled at me often; once in her breathless voice, she had asked me to carry a message to a friend, but that was all. I had, of course, never delivered the note. And a few months later, she was dead. Dead of a disease that no one would speak about — for it ate into her body, preying on her mind as quietly as it preyed on her cheek, robbing her of her wits, her youth, her beauty — till she was dead.

I had forgotten her then, after a week of inglorious tears that revealed my hidden feelings for all to see. I grew up in that week — but the note, it still lay folded into its little rectangle, somewhere. I looked at her who stood before me, her eyes searching my face and a great sadness overcame me. This too would pass, I knew, this love, and we too would pass, as my Jenny had done, beyond the whispering trees into a night where there was no sound.

She caught my look even in the light of the moon. And before I could ask her why she had spoken of Jenny, how she had discovered her grave, she reached out and held my hands tight in hers. I could feel her nails digging into my flesh — yet I stood suspended between two words — hesitating.

"She was beautiful, wasn't she?" she whispered and, before I could wonder how she knew, she was bent again over the stone, brushing away the leaves with one hand.

"Yes," I murmured. "Once I loved her too!" Then I awoke with a start. She stared up at me, her eyes floating in the wet of unshed tears. "Is that why you meet me here?" she asked.

Tenderness swept over me; how she must have suffered over the evening! I bent to lift her, to console her, but she moved away. "Show her to me," she cried, "Show me — I must see..." and her hands beat at the cold grave — an impatient knocking.

I caught her then, for I knew she had been scared out of her wits, by what I did not know, could not guess. I resolved very definitely to find another place, a quieter one, less haunted; for now the garden held a ghost for me. "Let us leave," I said, "let us leave this place and walk into the light. I shall never make you wait again."

But she held her head bent against me, crying softly. Her tears wet my shirt, and chilled my breast. I kissed her hair, it smelt strangely of flowers — wild flowers and dust and the haunting fragrance of lavender.

I touched her face, her wet, wet face, and forced her to look at me. Her eyes were dark, but a light reflected off them into mine. I could not fathom the strangeness of her look, and suddenly, the wind in the trees made me shiver.

The night had grown quiet, the music had died down and even the dull murmur of prayer had stilled into silence. "Come, my love, let us leave," I murmured. She moved softly, in step with me. "Come Sheila," I coaxed leading her onto the broken pathway, past the silver trunks of the sentinel trees that reached into the night.

She laughed a strange laugh – a throaty sound I had not heard before.

She twined her fingers firmly around my hand, nails biting into my skin again, and moved alongside. "Yes," she said, "But not Sheila. Jennifer."

17

TOO LATE FOR AMENDS

I DISCOVERED a terrible truth today. I discovered that Binabai is my mother. I am flesh of her brown servant class flesh, blood of her blood. My fair skin and delicate features are not proof of my upper class parentage, only one of life's little ironies. I must make amends, must repair the terrible damage I have done to her. Ma, your son is returning to you. After it is too late. Memories are painful things. But I must remember. Trace back the lines of my life, and see it with her eyes. To realise why she did what she did, to understand this strangely wonderful woman who is my mother.

I am eight years old when I first hear that Binabai is not my mother. A classmate of mine, Kishore, tells me one day, during one of our daily brawls. Binabai is not your mother. She is your servant, an *ayah*. Your parents died suddenly in an accident leaving you behind. Binabai tended you back with her care. She was alone too, a widow, childless. You were her greatest treasure. And nobody else wanted you. So she appealed to the state and adopted you. In fact, you are not a Maharashtrian, but a Punjabi. This is the gist of what Kishore tells me. When the teachers pull us apart, Kishore's nose is bleeding. I run home to Binabai and cling to her, shouting Ma, Ma, Ma.

It is Rajan's birthday. Three days before my birthday. In three days' time, I will be 12. I am dressed in the new clothes Ma has bought me for the occasion. I clutch my present for Rajan under one arm as I pull Ma's hand with the other, insisting that she should come along too. Everyone's parents have been invited. Why should Ma stay back? Rajan knows we are poor, I cry. Come, you must come. Ma gives in reluctantly and goes in to change her clothes.

At the party, I realise how different Ma is from the other boys' mothers. They are fair, slim, beautiful, smelling of sweet smells. Ma looks out of place in her bright pink nylon sari. She sits silent, far away from the rest of the ladies. Why don't you mix, Ma? Why is your skin so brown or ugly? I never realised before how sloppy she looks. She was right, she should have stayed at home.

I am so upset by these realisations that I refuse to have a party on my birthday. I don't want my friends to stare at Ma again!

Memories. Memories... what else can I do but relive them?

I do not know when the change occurred. But one day I realise I have begun to think of this mother who has brought me up, as Binabai, instead of Ma.

I do not let her know it. She may not be my mother, but she has certainly taken her place. I continue to speak the word that has no identity now. Ma has become a painless synonym of Binabai.

College... the thrill of being independent, of being free with lecturers, of talking to girls. I am quite a dashing young man, so my classmates say. I have typical Punjabi looks – fair skin, clear eyes, black hair. And good height. I am proud of myself. Today, I have taken on a job. A part-time teaching job, in an evening school. Binabai's meagre allowance, saved from her earnings from the vegetable shop, does not allow me to date girls. I have piled up fantastic bills at the college canteen. And a job is the only way of paying them off. Besides, clothes cost a lot and a guy must be well-dressed; specially if he is as popular with the girls as I am.

Binabai is happy for me – utterly unselfish as ever. She asks me for nothing. I give her nothing. She is content to remain as she is, and naturally so. Which *ayah* can boast of such a promising 'son'?

I have told Binabai today that I'm moving to a small flat. Rent Rs. 395. It is difficult to face my friends when they insist on visiting me at home. I've put them off too many times and they are getting suspicious that I have something to hide. Binabai refuses to leave her home. She prefers to live in the cramped two-room hut in that terrible locality. But she encourages me to move. Her eyes blur with happiness. I am relieved and yet just a bit sorry. She is happy. Her caterpillar has turned into a butterfly, and must seek its home in a flower garden! If only I had realised.

Memories! Today, the web has broken. The web I had built around myself has crumbled away. The jewels that glistened on the gossamer were only drops of water shining in the sun. I am no powerful builder of webs, only a dirty fly. Trapped forever.

Kirtibai, the old *dahiwali* who lives next door to Binabai's hut, comes running over. Binabai has been knocked down by a truck. Quite near my house. It seems she walked the six kilometres between our houses every day only to catch a glimpse of me to reassure herself that I was happy. And I never knew it. How could I? She never knocked on my door, fearing one of my friends would see her. Today, while she was walking back, a lorry struck her down. A crowd had gathered; and carried her, unconscious, moaning to herself, to the hospital. Kirtibai's eyes fill as she tells me all this. And now *beta*, let me break my vow of silence, now that only god knows whether Binabai will live, she says. And out comes the terrible tale... the drowning cascade of truth that has left me bereft of words and feeling. Robbed me of everything at one stroke.

I am Binabai's child. And a bastard at that. Binabai's master seduced her, while she was a servant at his house. He made promises of marriage. Binabai was fooled till she became pregnant. When he realised she was pregnant, he gave her a few hundred rupees for an abortion, and turned her out. He shut his door and mind to her.

Binabai refused to have an abortion. She tried to burn herself to death; her parents saved her. They nursed her to health, and, after I was born, coaxed her into sending me to an orphanage. Then she could marry again, they said. No one would know of her sin.

Binabai had listened. And waited. One night, when I was about a year old, she slipped out of the house with me. And moved to another town – this town. Kirtibai had befriended her and helped her set up her vegetable shop.

Binabai had made up her lie about my parentage because she did not want her son to be a servant. Her handsome son, who looked so much like his father, must give up her way of life, must grow into a *sahib*. And only a lie could make that happen. So Binabai created a lie.

It is all over now, Binabai is dead. Perhaps it is for the best. She died happy, fulfilled; her years of self-denial rewarded. Perhaps it would have broken her heart if she had lived and known I knew the truth. I'd have forced her to live with me; and her sacrifice would have been in vain. My friends, my position, my prospects would have all disappeared with her appearance. And the years of self-denial, the years of suppressed motherhood, choked by her own doing, would have been nullified. Memories... I shift the screen of memories away. The past is over. I have learnt a great lesson. Truth is mighty, powerful to face; I am blasted by the encounter. And yet I cannot make amends for the sins of my heart. Let me at least give Binabai – Ma – her due.

I shall keep her secret in my heart – till it grows through my conscience and devours me. That will be my only atonement.

18
THE SEVEN-CORNERED TABLE

"PAPA, I DON'T want Mini to sit next to me."

"Papa, Papa – tell Mini to be quiet, I will sit at the table. Papa – how will we sit on the chairs? They are too high."

Ever since we laid eyes on the table – there had been no end to their excitement. Nandita saw it first. "Look Papa, such a lovely table. Papa – it's got seven sides." I pulled Mini away from the tiny China desk she was trying her best to touch, and turned to look at the table.

It stood there almost beckoning me to buy it. Take us home – the lions at the ends of the curved legs seemed to purr, cat-like. And when Mini promptly put a finger into one of the open mouths and squealed in delighted terror, I thought for a moment, it had clamped shut... A beauty of a table. I had expected to get a functional cheap but sturdy table for my trio to study at, but this was temptation indeed.

Nothing I had seen in China Bazaar with its dizzying curios and what have you, prepared me for this treasure. It stood out, even among the alabaster statuettes and carved wooden sideboards, claiming instant attention. The gleaming polish of its surface reflected the brass kitsch strewn over the shop – almost mockingly. This was, I knew, definitely a table with personality.

Normally, I am a mundane man. Bringing up three daughters, motherless and scatter-brained as they are, is a full-time job – and when one is a professor with a bunch of onion-headed students to face every morning – there is little time for life's finer moments. True, when Ruma was alive, we used to be more particular about taking time off for 'romancing,' as she called it. We'd saunter into museums, or art galleries, linger at an auction holding each other's hands safely to prevent any false moves. And once in a year, we'd splurge on a purchase – a rolltop desk, that oil painting at half price – they were the only mementos left of my happier days. And my three daughters, of course. Harum-scarum girls – always fighting and squalling – only Nandita had some of her mother's quiet dignity and her love of beauty. No wonder she had spotted the table.

For Ruma's sake – as much as for mine – I decided to buy the table. It would do well as the study table, I told myself – each girl can have two sides – and there will still be one surface area to spare. I'd have to get low chairs for them to sit on – for the present, straw mats would do. If only Mini and Bulbul would stop fighting, I could find out how much it cost.

Surprisingly, it did not cost the earth; less than one of these steel and sunmica things I'd inspected earlier on anyway. Of course, the shopkeeper noticed my interest and started by demanding all my month's salary – but I had noticed the deep scar on the face of the table, and played it up to advantage. My advantage of course – for the price dropped, slowly but steadily to affordable levels.

I ignored the squealing voices and questions, and

concentrated on making the table feel at home. To me, it was the VIP of the year – as all our past indulgences had been. I had to make it feel special – to feel special myself. Just looking at it would make me glow for months! I think I missed Ruma most in the moments I placed the table, just so, in the girls' room – with the light hanging over it, dead centre. How pricey it looked. The impact was priceless!

And when the three dark heads bowed over it, and the shoulders bent forward, and the little wrists pushed pencils over the pages – the tableau was complete. I felt a rush of love flooding my throat – tasting suspiciously of tears. The table was symbolic of my home – perfect – except for the deep flaw. The one missing portion.

I looked up from my desk to see Nandita framed in the doorway. The light fell on her hair – giving her a halo – and the way the shadows framed her face made her look suddenly more mature. My breath held for a second. My ten-year-old was a beauty in the making – another Ruma! She looked uncertain so I bade her to enter. The child was growing up; her earlier boisterousness was being replaced by a strong quiet. Perhaps it would shield her from the buffeting of the adolescent years ahead of her.

"Papa – the table shakes too much again." Her voice broke into my thoughts, and I reached out and touched her head in some typically protective gesture.

"The table, Papa," she repeated, "Mini shakes it so much – I cannot write at it." I sighed. Mini – boisterous, quick tempered, incorrigible Mini – I could imagine her making the most of the table's in-built wobble. Nudge, nudge, she would go, of course – giggling inside herself – waiting for Nandi to start writing again before she leaned casually and bore down on the table again. Nudge.

Well, there was some disciplining necessary. So I got

up to scold the errant child. But Nandita stopped me. "She does it only to tease me, Papa, she's such a baby. Can you make the table stop shaking?" I promised I would – that Sunday. Meanwhile, Nandita said, she would work at the dining table again. Till Sunday.

But Sunday and after, the table continued to wobble. Nandita continued to work at the dining table. And Mini lost a target for her persecution.

It didn't take her long to find another target though. With Nandita away, Mini concentrated on Bulbul. Often as I worked on my lecture notes, the sound of their chatter would reach my ears, and I'd sneak across in my slippers to spy on them. They presented a pretty sight, huddled over the table, giggling conspiratorially – but that was no way to get homework done.

Suddenly, one day, I had had enough. "Mini," I roared, all the anger of forced single parenthood in my voice, "that is enough. Now get up from there."

Bulbul trembled visibly at my voice, but Mini, brazen as ever, looked up, her plaits flying in defiance. "Papa, we were only laughing over Bulbul's textbook lesson." I froze my melting heart, look her hand in mine, swept up her books in one regal sweep with the other and marched her off into the living room.

"Here, you sit here and study. *Didi* will keep an eye on you," and I placed her book at the end of the rectangle, opposite Nandi's. That would be all for the present. Chastened, Mini would play safe for at least the next few days. My velvet-hearted daughters hated my iron-fisted role almost as much as I did.

The table soon became part of the family. We relaxed the VIP treatment a little – and one measure of our acclimatisation to it was the fact that, often in the day, a book or a glass would be seen on top of it. Quite homely — part of the family.

Mini mentioned it the moment the girls entered the house. It was one of my half days, and I was relaxing over a cup of tea, when the girls tumbled out of the rickshaw. Mini rushed in, voice decibels above endurance, crying. "Papa, Papa, Bulbul's teacher has sent a letter for you. Sealed letter, Papa, all closed and stuck. She licked it shut," she added, her voice lowering with the seriousness of the crime.

"Let me see," I quietened her, "first, you change and have your tea." Bulbul handed me the letter as she went in, looking somewhat tense and strained. It made me wonder what had happened in school — nothing serious, I was sure — Bulbul was the scholar in the family. Very industrious, a bit slow perhaps — but essentially industrious.

The note was terse, to the point; school teachers hadn't changed over the years obviously. "Mr. Banerjee (it read), Could you please make it convenient to visit me during school hours next week to discuss your daughter Rajashree's performance in class? Please do come." Make it convenient — I smiled at the phrase. As if parents had a choice when a class teacher called.

***

Father, mother, mentor now. How many roles can I play? Somewhere in all my role playing, something has gone wrong — and likely too. Without a prompter, the best actor will somewhere muff up his lines — and I'm only a professor of humanities. Sitting in the doctor's waiting room, I realised with a start that Bulbul had indeed changed a lot. She was quieter, for one. Perhaps I had noticed it only in the relief it gave to my ears – and not recognised it as a cause for alarm. But looking at her fragile form beside me, on the rexine covered sofa, I realised the child had lost weight too. More alarming, there were soft smudges under her eyes – and a furrow gathered her brow. She started up when I spoke to her; guiltily, a bit scared. I knew her timidity was partly due to fear partly over this visit to the doctor – but even then, the start was almost unexpectedly severe.

But the doctor seemed quite unperturbed. He looked long and seriously at the notebook I had brought along with me, examining the careening script as it rushed across the page in no orderly direction. He stared at Bulbul as if he would look beyond that curved forehead into the very recesses of her brain. Then, sitting back in his executive chair, he chatted with us both quite as if we were there on a social visit.

"Do you feel any strain in reading?" he asked Bulbul. I started to reply – but he stopped me with one raised finger and continued to look at my daughter. Bulbul shook her head slowly. "No," she said, in a tiny voice. "Do you find your mind wandering in class?" he asked – very casually again.

Bulbul nodded, but when she did not speak, I urged her to speak up. "I hear too many people talking sometimes," she said, "when teacher gives dictation, I cannot make out which is her voice."

Perhaps that explained it – some kind of aural hallucination, plus a wobbly table, plus growing up motherless and being the middle child – I felt strange emotions pull at me – relief, retreat, love. But the doctor brushed aside my fears, for once. While Bulbul waited in the room outside, he perched himself on the edge of the table to dispel my fatherly anxiety. "It's nothing to worry about, really," he said, British manner curling at the edge to reveal his Indianness. "If I were you, I'd watch her a little more closely than the other two girls. Let her mix with them more, let her feel no anxiety over performance. And that wobbly table," he added, looking at me in much the same way I look at Mini when she refuses her bedtime milk, "I suggest you use it for something other than writing. However," he added in a softer tone, "if a month of this therapy shows no improvement, maybe we should consult a child psychologist." My face must have changed colour at his words, for he thumped me heartily on the shoulder and said, "She'll be fine, old man, don't worry. Some girls have more growing pains than others."

Truly enough, Bulbul improved with a little special attention. Her sisters rallied around her beautifully, making her the centre of attention, giving her little surprise gifts. Mini showed her softer side, she was Ruma's daughter after all. Each morning she would wake up a little earlier than Bulbul and steal out of the room to snip a tiny flower from the backyard. A wild daisy, one day; a bunch of colourful bougainvillea, another day. But when Bulbul woke, the flower would stand by her bedside, and Mini too, grinning broadly. Evening times, I stretched with relief to hear the familiar giggling around the dining table – and even serious little Nandita joining in instead of hushing them up. Our family had ridden the crisis well – and now we went back to being ourselves – outings at the zoos on Sundays or taking evening walks together after dinner. Father, mother, mentor, counsellor – I thought, but did not mind one bit. What were daughters for, if not to be pampered?

But what was to be done with the table? It had scarcely

spent six months of its year-long term as VIP purchase, and was already being superannuated! Ruma would not have let that happen. I made another attempt. Heaving and pushing, we shifted the table to my room. Very generously, Mini offered her stool for me to sit on, when I worked at the table. That was that, the table was my 'baby' now – and I would tend it and use it, and make it mine.

    I did not expect it to be quite so unstable though. As if with a new found freedom of expression, it wobbled and shook at the slightest pressure. Writing on it was an exercise – it took all of my self-control to make sure my hand did not go skidding madly across the sheet. When I finally gave up trying to write, and set my books down to read – I felt one of the lions had flared its mouth in a smile. The quirk of fancy persisted; but looking closely, I knew it was a trick of lighting. And my own tired mind, of course. No more Chor Bazaar purchases, I promised myself. They fall short of perfection. As I rose to leave the table for my bed, the deep scar caught my eye again. The polish gleamed dull and, in the light, the burnished mahogany in the heart of the scar seemed like a pool of liquid bronze. Almost like blood, I thought, then stopped short. I must be getting senile surely. I told myself, to discover a penchant for the macabre at 40-plus!

***

    I was at the table when Mickey dropped in. Mickey is an old friend – the kind who grows with you, through college, and marriage and into old age. Dependable, no-nonsense type – Ruma used to say he was good for me. "Mickey is one person who can draw you out, and not even let you notice it," she used to say. We've had fun times together, the Banerjees and bachelor Mickey. Never a false note, never a shadow of discord. Yet, in his own way, Mickey kept his distance too. He travelled a lot, and there were months when I'd have no word from him. Then suddenly, he would walk in, as if it was a daily habit, hand in pocket, asking loudly, "Where is everybody? Mickey is here."

He walked straight into my room – and before he had really seen me, noticed the table. "That's nice, how much did they charge you for it?" he asked. Typically Mickey, so direct. I told him and he whistled. "Cheap," he said – "What's the catch?" I told him about the scar and how it had helped the bargain. "But that's not all," I added, "The table is practically useless for the purpose I got it – it wobbles." "Pack it," Mickey advised. I challenged him to do so, and he tore up odd bits of paper and cardboard covers off notebooks to pack under the table leg. I sat back and let him mutter under his breath as the table won every round. Wobble, it would go, wobble – each wobble, more triumphant than the last.

At last, he pushed away a damp slick of hair from his eyes and straightened up. "It's useless," he said – "The table's all wrong." He hadn't quite finished with it though. "If you press down with your elbow, you should be able to write, you know," he added, and set up a demonstration.

It was pointless of course. He would hardly move his pen across the page, when the table would dip suddenly. Then, as he settled down to write at that angle, the table would shift again, gathering its strength as it were, to resist that punishing elbow.

Two attempts and Mickey had had enough. 'That's it," he said, throwing pen and paper down on the table with finality. "I think the table is alive." I laughed at his statement – the sheer absurdity of the discovery tickled me. Of course, it was alive. All our VIP purchases were alive; things that breathed and belonged – things to be treated with attention, even respect. I told him as much. But Mickey brushed aside my little speech. "I mean it's alive, idiot; possessed. There's a spirit around." Hard stuff to swallow, but I sailed along. I had learned to take the path of least resistance with Mickey.

"Listen, let's hold a séance," he said. "We'll get to the bottom of this mystery." That was really going over the falls – I demurred. "With young girls at home," I murmured, "calling spirits and all that is taboo – who knows, if one of them should attract a spirit!"

"Bosh, man," Mickey's eyes shone with excitement. "Let's try it out – we'll be pioneers I bet – and solve a century-old riddle perhaps!" He rubbed his palms in anticipation. "I've never conducted a séance before, but you'll be a receptive medium – you sensitive types usually are… It's settled then," he said, stalking out of the room. "We'll send your girls to a film on Saturday night and set the scene." And before my protest could find a voice, he was out of the house.

Saturday night, I was ill-prepared. Mentally at least. However, knowing Mickey's impetuousness, I took all precautions. I sent the girls off to a film show, much to their surprise. And sat down and waited.

Mickey walked in with his usual nonchalance. Calm as ever – but under the surface, I could feel the tightening of muscles. "Will you have some tea?" I asked him, hoping to set a domestic note to the scene and make him forget the purpose of this visit. Fat chance. "Are the girls out of the way?" he asked, then before I could answer, "No, I don't want tea – let's get down to business."

I could swear the curtains in my room billowed

ominously at his words – but then, if I could see wooden lion faces smiling, I could see anything. Yet, even as we set the table and lit the candle, a strange notion took hold of me. It was a tremendous fear, not unmixed with anticipation. I noticed my hands were trembling – but I quietened myself with the observation that so were Mickey's.

When the lights were switched off, the room seemed to get visibly colder. I shivered a tiny tremble, and set to the business at hand. Mickey lit the candle, and invoked the spirit. 'Whoever you are, come," he said "we are ready for you. We will do your bidding – release you from your torture. Come." There was no response. I felt the cold tremor again, and my eyes stared into the darkness beyond the pale of candle light. Nothing. Mickey incanted again. "Come," he ended. "Come!" his voice echoed through the darkness, and I heard him draw his breath in sharply – "Come," he said more softly – and the echo sounded back as a reverberating hum. And I felt the table move – nudge – one small nudge. I felt my finger grip the pen so hard, I was sure the stem would snap. But the table nudged again and I let the pen move whichever way it would, powerful forces seemed to work in that moment, the table moved jerkily, once, twice – then again – a pause, and the darkened room. Then again my hand moved the pen along the paper. I felt some tremendous pressure forcing my hand to write – an overenthusiastic teacher guiding a learner's pencil – and my fingers ached with tension.

The nudge again, and yet once more – the drama went on till I lost count of time – endlessly. As suddenly – it was still again – warmer even, for I felt my fingers touch my palm and it was clammy. We sat for a while in the moving darkness, mesmerised by the candle – and then Mickey moved to switch on the light. There, under my hand, lay the sheet of paper I had used and, on it, and in a jagged writing – a desperate hand had written out the letters M-U-R-D-E-R, then a space, and another word 'Revenge.' The last letter of the word trailed off out of the page and I noticed my pen had marked the polished wood, deeply. I had never known such strength – the wood was carved.

We mused over the séance for a while, then Mickey snapped out of the mood. "Well, that explains your wobbly table," he said in a normal voice, though his eyes held a strange look. Despite himself, he had been scared out of his wits. I opened the cupboard and pulled out my bottle of rum and fixed us a drink each, this was one way to get out of the evening's mood. But Mickey continued to ponder over the séance. "You must find out whom the table belonged to," he said," And effect a revenge?" I asked; life had quite prepared me for any statement from Mickey. But he only shook his head. "You must find out to know completely what is half revealed," he said. "But you must get rid of the table." I swallowed my drink in quick long draughts and breathed deeply; my friend was not insane after all.

***

We found the shop quite easily. And accosted the shopkeeper. The boy first looked blankly at us – then, as we badgered him for information, he unwound a little. We pressed our advantage, assuring him we were only curious, and Mickey's deftly handed ten-rupee note finally unleashed the story. The table had a history, the boy knew that. It made for unrest in the homes it went to, the boy knew that too. In the house of its previous owner, the lady of the house had had a mental breakdown – the table was being used by her at that time. But he did not know the cause. No, he did not know who the first owner of the table was. "I only know that I bought the table with a truck of things from an auction," he said "it was a bulk purchase. The table was old and scarred, but beautiful, so I polished it well and sold it. For a handsome price. But within two months, the man brought it back and sold it to me at half the price. He hated the table, he said. I thought he was mad, sahib. I took it back. But, each time I sold the table it came back. Last time, the mad lady's husband threatened to have the police on me – said I did *jadoo tona*, and sold stolen goods. So, I wanted to cut up the table and use the legs for making something else – a sofa perhaps. Then, you came along and bought it. And who am I to disappoint a customer?"

Well, that was the dead end of the mystery. I wanted to hold another séance, to discover who had been murdered and why? Was the scar on the table made by the instrument that struck the deathly blow, I wondered. Evenings, I would stare at the table and imagine a hazy figure slumped across it, blood lapping at its outlines, Mickey held my imagination in check. "What will you gain if you solve the mystery?" he demanded. "Only a troubled mind. Do you want to spend your life hunting out a killer who may even be dead? Even if he isn't, who will believe you? How will you track him down?"

I retreated under the force of his logic. It took some explaining, but the girls agreed to the return of the table. Nandi looked at it sadly with her round eyes, but said nothing. But Mini wanted to come along. "Let's get something else instead," she said. "I'll come and help you choose."

I put them off firmly, and went with the cartman to Chor Bazaar. The boy was silent and low in spirit – he helped me unload the table and, without a word, counted my money out and handed it to me.

I left Chor Bazaar with a heavy heart. As if I had abandoned a friend. As I turned the corner of the road, I looked back. The table stood outside the shop – looking as distinctive as ever. To me it seemed, even from the distance, that the lion legs looked somewhat different. Instead of the smugness they usually wore, their cat faces seemed tense and expectant in an attitude of waiting!

19
TRAM RIDER

THE NIGHT WAS shattered by a moon which shamed the lamps that burned bravely through the haze of mist that veiled them. The cobbled stones of the pavement outside the imposing station that let trains in and out of Milan wore a dark look of brooding, except when the dew on them caught the light of passing cars now and then.

It was not the best of times for a woman to stand waiting for a tram, especially since the station clock showed eleven, but there I was, doing just that. The only thing that mitigated my sense of trepidation was the fact that opposite me, on the other side of the tram lines, there was a crowd, of decent looking men and women, also waiting.

I looked around quickly, and took stock of my own partners in waiting. Two old men, and a seedy tramp, smoking a cigarette. Not bad, I told myself, I cannot come to much harm from them.

It was a thought too soon. Even as I watched entranced, he came, looking much like a hero from a B grade Italian film... all brawn and swagger, his muscles rippling on his arm, the tee shirt he wore a mockery of the cold air that, even as I watched him, made me draw my coat closer

TRAM RIDER

around me. He walked up and stood in line with the men, then leaned forward and pulled the still unlit cigarette out of the mouth of the third man... who stared at him in anger, and a certain air of helplessness.

I did not wait to see more. I could hear the sound of the tram approaching on the opposite side, and crossed the road. It was, to my utmost relief, the tram I wanted, a 33, and though it was going the wrong way, I jumped in, along with the rest of the waiting crowd. Sooner or later, I said, it would turn back and go my way. And a warm, well lit tram was any day better than waiting outside.

Again, a thought too soon. With the air of a King Kong wresting open the gates of hell, he pulled open the tram's fragile wooden doors, and stepped in. I drew back into the seat... and watched fascinated as he took his, on the side opposite me.

Luckily, he seemed lost in some reverie. Not for long, though. He got up in a rush, and moved to the driver's cabin, and spoke to him. The driver answered back. From the tone of the words, I surmised that he was asking if the tram would go his way, and was being given an answer in the negative. Ah, I thought, he will get off now. Not that he had bothered me in any way, it was just the look of him that spelt danger to my mind, and indeed even as he turned and strode back to his seat, I realised my instincts were correct.

He sat himself down, and turned to glare at the rest of the passengers. Most of them avoided him with studied care, but all the same he picked on a young man opposite and made a few rude gestures. Muttering all the time to himself, he would suddenly raise his voice and speak to whoever his gaze rested on. Then, finding no response, he banged his hand against the shut windows, causing the glass to sing, and making the lighting in their fluted glass holders blaze just that bit brighter for that moment.

Meanwhile the car sped on into the night. We had, I noticed, left the brighter section, and gone into some seedier part of Milan, where the roads were lined with sad hotels and neon lights that proclaimed their names in an anaemic blue. At almost every stop, people were getting off with amazing alacrity. I was not sure whether it was because they had reached their destination, or due to their need to avoid the beast in the tram.

Beast he was, at least in temperament. Some demon paced his mind, and he would articulate its thoughts with violent expletives, and bang his fist into the window. I was sure at one moment that he would crash through the glass and find his fist covered in blood, but the glass held miraculously.

I looked at him more with curiosity than with fear. His pants were boot cut, his belt was of the finest leather, he had silver studs in his ears, and over one eyebrow. And his face, when it was at peace, which was only in fleeting moments, was that of a handsome man, who could well have found a role in a Hindi film.

Maybe he was on drugs because he was thwarted in his desire for fame, maybe it was the lack of riches that made him bitter… I thought… till finding him staring straight into my face as I stared back at him, I quickly lowered my gaze and looked with deep interest at my shoes. He lurched up from his seat. I could feel his shadow looming over me, and uttered a prayer for succour, but he turned with a sudden movement and went off towards the driver to harangue him again. I worried then, when the driver spoke to him, with sharp words, that he would fell him with a blow, and we would all be stranded there.

TRAM RIDER

The car, I noticed had reached a u-turn, and I hoped at last that the ghostly journey would end. There were still four people besides the beast, as I had already nicknamed him, in the tramcar, and I wanted to believe that the return journey would be brighter, without the beast, and with a new clutch of passengers travelling from the dark regions we had reached, into the light.

And then, it happened. We were approaching a traffic light, which turned red. He stood up from the seat he had sunk into again, and lurched towards the driver. He bent over him, and I swear for one horrific moment that I saw a fang red with blood, as he spoke to the man.

The driver opened the car doors, started the tram, almost as if he had not noticed the threat that loomed over him, then even as the car started, doors still open, he jammed the brakes. I watched horrified as the man, who had stood framed against the darkness, swayed for one interminably long moment in the jerk and fell right out of the car, through the open doors, into the night.

Without missing a beat, the driver released the handle that shut the doors and started off, speeding into the night. I sat, unable to speak a word, looking now at the driver, and now at the other passengers, who seemed not to have noticed anything at all. I turned my head to see what had befallen the beast, as he fell out of the tram. And saw, a sight that can even today, when I think of it, chill my very bones.

There, loping after us, in a jagged run, was the beast, furry, huge, the tee shirt still around his shoulders, his legs moving at a gallop as he seemed to move in. I distinctly saw the fangs I had thought I had imagined, and stuck out of his head were definitely not human...

And then, we turned the corner, and as we entered

the lighted street, he came closer, and vanished. Vanished as in... poof... One minute he was there, loping behind the tram, looking as if he would clamber in and vanquish all within, the next moment, poof, he was gone.

I stared at the darkness behind. There was nothing. I stared at the others in the car, they looked lost in their own thoughts. Had I imagined it after all? I sat very silent and invisible through the rest of the trip, and got off at my stop.

The next day, I recounted the incident to my Italian friend... told him I had probably drunk a stronger wine on the train than I was used to handling, and that it had resulted in this rather strange experience. He looked at me strangely. "What time did you say you caught your tram?" he asked... "11," I answered. He shook his head, and pulled out a timetable. "The 33," he said, unfolding the sheet and pointing to the relevant column, "never runs beyond 10 o'clock. They discontinued it because of the murders that would happen on that particular route..." Seeing my stare, he continued in a softer tone, "night after night, a year ago, passengers would be mutilated by some unknown killer... You must be mistaken," he said, "there is no way you could have taken that tram. I do believe the wine went to your head, after all."

"It must have," I muttered. "But then, how did I reach my stop? Since no other tram connects the station to my hotel."

He did not have an answer to that. And neither have I found one till date.

20
THE LOST NOTE

THE SHRILL, SHARP voice of the flute finally woke him. He had been listening to it for a while – it seemed to come from the far distance, through the hills, past the mists – a plaintive note that carried a bit of chill with it. Or so it seemed to him. Then it pierced through his consciousness and he awoke.

He realised with a start that he had been sleeping. And they must be all ready. Waiting. Waiting for him. He jumped up from the black backed chair, with white lettering on it that said DIRECTOR; and pulled on his jacket. He would never have dared to sit on that chair before; let alone sleep on it – but he had over the years begun to belong. And once in a while was allowed a liberty or two. Sleeping while they waited was not one of them.

He opened the door, and walked quickly past the empty studio, through the long, cold corridors. Hurrying, hurrying. Long years of hard work, of endless dedication, of faithfulness to his muse and her masters had finally found for him a permanent place with the music group. His flute had woven its magic on them; woven itself into every tune they created. Krishna, they called him in jest – we cannot think of a hit without our little Krishna. He bowed, as much to their collective love as to the fact that he was so much younger — and accepted their nickname. His name was not Krishna. But they were right about one thing. Since his flute had joined its music to theirs, the hits had come fast and hard on each other's heels. Unwinding like a spiral of smoke, rising from a woodfire. Unending as the road that leads a weary traveller homewards. The music director loved him. "My Krishna," he'd say, "come take your place; and let me hear how this piece sounds on your flute." If the others felt any envy or rancour, they never showed it. He was part of them; part of their music. Their success. The line up of awards proved it. Though none was his or bore his name, all the awards belonged to him. As much to the director. They agreed on it, without ever talking about it even once. He was their lucky charm.

He came up short against the recording studio. The red light was on — the heavy door, cushioned on the inside, was shut tight. The usual piles of footwear stood deferentially outside, unworthy of the hallowed air within.

His heart missed a beat! Had they started without him? He stood hesitant at the door, one hand at the handle. But not pulling at it. He couldn't disturb a recording. He willed it to open, to his surprise, the red glow that had lit his face vanished. He looked up, the light was off. Quick as a bird, he lifted his arm and tugged at the door. It yielded, to his relief. He wasn't locked out any more. Inside, the lights blazed in tiny spots from the ceiling. He stood for a minute — a long second — taking in a picture he'd never really seen clearly before, because he'd always been a part of it.

They sat there, the musicians, at their appointed places. The light focused like points on the instruments making brass look like gold; steel look like molten silver. He could feel the cold of the metal in the squat drums, their tops tight against the edges, awaiting the feel of the drummer's fingers.

His hand tightened around his flute – he could feel the cold steel of it warm under his touch. Soon, it would moan under his breath, then sing in ecstasy. Taking a deep breath, he stepped in. The music director looked up at him from his notes. "You're late," he said, a faint rebuke curling at the edge of his voice. His heart sank again. He hated being rebuked. Hated being late.

"I'm sorry, I... fell asleep," and he stammered and hurried to his yet vacant seat. The mike hung loose and disused; were they going on without him after all? He shut the thought, and the panic it brought to his stomach, firmly away, and pulled the mike up and fixed it in position. The flute throbbed against his palm; it was time for its magic to unfurl.

He watched the other instrumentalists warily, covertly, through eyes bent as if to examine his flute, they were looking towards him, but not at him. That was their way of showing their disapproval.

He knew he was guilty. He had absconded from rehearsals one whole day on a whim. Then, when he had snapped out of it, he had realised it was too late to catch up. They had moved studios and no one knew quite where they had gone.

It had taken him all the week to locate them – and then, he'd sent a written apology and begged to be forgiven. He knew the whim was only his pride, trying to prove to himself his power over the group. His power to make or break a song. To create or mar a hit.

THE LOST NOTE

They had been generous. There were no rebukes; no refusal to let him be back. He had been at the time of their last rehearsals; and the recording that would follow immediately. Studio No : 3, 4 p.m. sharp. And yet, perversely or perhaps, half afraid, he had lounged around through the afternoon watching the shooting in the studio shed next door, till he'd fallen fast asleep! And now, he'd come bumbling in, as if he had not a worry. No wonder they were angry!

He sent out a smile – of apology. Abject apology. The eyes, one by one, locked away, wrapped up, lost in their respective instruments, they seemed not to notice him, his dove of reconciliation fluttered and died at his feet.

The note uncurled itself and spread like a mist. The musicians looked up. He could see he had won them over; their anger melting like snow in the warmth of his notes. Their backs relaxed, their throats permitted a swallow of emotion; and then the smiles lit the room. "You rascal," the violinist said peering with moist eyes from behind his instrument. "Where the devil were you all this while?"

"Doesn't matter – now that he's back, let's start," said the tabla player, but he knew from the gruffness that the man was moved.

"Next time, we won't be so ready to forgive," – it was the music director's voice – and he snapped to attention. He never risked rousing his temper – there was too much at stake.

"Let's start," the music director said. The static in the air almost hit him again; the moment of waiting, of knowing that in two seconds, in one. Now, it would be time to set out. To begin. And take off on yet another journey with the Muse.

"One, two – go –" and he glanced quickly at his notes to see that he went on at the end of the first movement. His body tense as a violin string, he waited. The music flowed like a dream around him. It became a river, beating against his skin, permeating it, filling his senses. He floated with it, almost drowning in the joy of its rise and fall.

Only his mind remained alert, crouched, waiting to bounce on the moment when he must put his breath into this flute and join in. The moment came close. He lifted the flute to his mouth and waited. Now – he let out his breath, blowing gently, as the composition demanded. The silence filled the room as the music stopped. He had played it wrong. Instead of the flowing lilt that was expected of him, he had managed only a shrill, sharp note. Plaintive, even sickly. And it had ruined the music completely.

He looked at the rest of the musicians, aghast. He never made mistakes. "Why then, let's try again;" the music director said. "Once more." He waited, tense and angry this time hardly hearing the music around him. His eyes were glued to his cue; his mind played the note he had to play, again and again.

And then, he lifted the flute to his lips and played it. Again the disarrayed note filled his heart with despair. The musicians looked at him, and played on; as if they had not heard. But the music director signalled to them to stop. The silence filled his senses, smashing against his heart and stretching the muscles of his throat! "Play it again," the music director said, still gently; he was amazed that the man hadn't got angry yet. He had been known to throw batons at players who could not pin down a tune the first time!

"Solo," the music director continued – as the others picked up their instruments. The light caught the steel and brass and slid across the room, as the instruments were lowered again.

He lifted his flute to his lips, listened to the note the music director hummed, read the notations on the page in front of him, and played. The note curled out in a wail. Gripping his throat with fear, filling his eyes with nameless dread.

"You've missed out on too much," the music director noted wryly. His voice was soft, too soft; as if he were musing to himself. Yet, there was no admonishment in it; so he felt heartened.

"Maybe you need to listen to the rest of the music, to find your place in it," the music director suggested. He nodded, relieved not to have to play that plaintive note again.

The musicians lifted their instruments and began to play. He listened, and in the magic of the music, he could hear quite, quite clearly, the wail of his flute. Loud, insistent, sharp and very discordant. "Stop it" – he cried, his voice shrieking with the pain of if. "Stop it whatever it is. Can't you hear it?"

The music director signalled for a stop. The music ceased. He turned to him and smiled. "We heard it the moment you walked in," he said. "It was you who wouldn't hear it. So I had to make you listen; to show you didn't belong."

"What is it?"–he asked. "What is it that I have done? Why can't I play it right? Please, please help me..." he was a little boy again, in front of his mother, who lay dying – and he was trying to revive her as she drooped heavy in his arms, too tiny, too weak to support her, too scared to drop her and let his legs run for help.

"Please help me," the helplessness engulfed him. "I want to play along with you again. Please. It's been so long."

The abyss of abandonment seemed to swallow him. He found himself crying. His arms stretched out, for support.

"Grandpa—wake up, you're crying in your sleep..." the voice went on and on, shaking him awake.

He opened his eyes, still wet with his despair and looked around. He saw the years in between stretch like a desert – dividing what had been from what was now. The musicians had long since left him, fading out one by one from his life. The music had been dead for an eon. It lived only in the records that played occasionally over the radio. Even his mind had stopped playing it for so long. He wondered what had made him remember – and whether the ache in his chest had anything to do with the memory. He lifted himself painfully, slowly from his bed. Moving across the room, he walked to the old curio case that stood against the wall. His grandchild watched while he opened the glass door and lifted the flute out from inside its dusty interior. The steel still shone silver, though specks of black seemed to have mottled it over the years. His hands trembled as he lifted the flute, and placed it against his lips.

His chest tightened as he blew gently. The note curled out pure and clean – beating with passion to land in perfect sync to the music he had heard in his sleep. He went back to the bed, his flute clutched tight in his palm, its steel warming to his touch, its magic melting into his skin and he lay down on his bed, and placed the flute on his chest.

And, like the smoke rising from a fire – a smile engulfed him, perfect understanding; he waited.

21

A GOOD WIFE

THREE NIGHTS in a row, she watched him, and she was sure. He was not an ordinary man, she had been fooled at first. The first night, she had woken up from a sleep that seemed to drag her into itself, a sleep full of dark sounds and ringing echoes. A light shone full through the smoke that filled the tunnel of her sleep, and grew steadily brighter. And brighter.

It hurt her eyes so. She flung her shut lids open to see him bent over her, staring. His look was fixed on her eyes. She shifted, and drifted off to sleep again.

She had been fooled that night. Not any more, not since she woke again, wild with a nameless fear, to disengage his arm from around her. He sighed, murmured and turned away. As he stretched a hand out, she caught the swish of fur and heard a wing beat just above her heart. The moment passed; but she was alert.

She slept little after that night, catching her sleep by day so she could watch. And know. And set her fears awing.

Covertly she had watched, her hand thrown, as if in

deep slumber, across her eyes. He awoke, he stared at her long and hard. She could sense his gaze from behind the dark curtain of her lids held stubbornly, achingly down. Then convinced that the sudden intake of her breath had been but a whim of sleep, he turned and stretched.

She watched him tonight, too, as he uncurled himself and stood along the wall. The air-conditioner gave a strange hiccup, and she knew he had thrown open the window. The moonlight padded in, flowing past the grills, around the net curtains that were exposed, now that he had pulled away the heavier drapes.

He drew himself up in the moonlight; his skin glistening a rich ebony as he bared his chest to the moon, throwing away the silken nightshirt that she had so lovingly embroidered for him as a wedding present. He threw his head back. And in the grey silver beam that lit his neck, she could see the sinews taut, the fur curling in elastic electricity.

He stretched his arms, and the webbing of his hands blotted out the moonlight. She closed her eyes, expecting his next move. For she knew he would turn for one last look at her, to ensure she was asleep. Then he'd turn, fold his arms close to his chest, and with a flutter, he'd be gone into the night.

She walked around the house, wondering where it was he went. What did he seek, she wondered, in the darkness of the night? Prey or succour? She walked a dream and wished she could wake from it. And even as the moon set, the night stilled, and the air conditioner laboured on without hope of respite, she found herself sinking, sinking into her tunnel of sleep. Sighing for release.

Mornings, he was always there, at her side. Face

innocent of deceit, body spent with his adventure, flung carelessly across the sheets. She watched the innocence of his curling lashes against his cheek as he slept and knew she had dreamed. Willed herself to believe she had dreamed.

And knew she hadn't.

She took it into her heart and held the secret. No one would know, not even he. After all, they had married for love, and she loved him. And hers it was to bear the burden of his secret. Hiding the knowledge even from he who knew it within himself.

She took precautions, though. Read up all she could about bats. Their habits, their preferences. The radar signals they followed, their weaknesses, as of sight. So, though by day she let him be a man, husband, provider and householder; at night, she took charge. Never letting him drive back after a party, never leaving him alone with children if any were around. Never, never letting him wander near the edge of a terrace, or under an overhanging bough. It wouldn't do to tempt him to break through and be his other self. She knew that. They were safe, the two of them, as long as he felt his secret was safe.

She read all she could about rabies. And deep in the recesses of her medicine chest, a vial of serum waited, just in case. And delving into even more complex writing on mythology, she learned to tell hostesses when she accepted an invitation for dinner, to make a few dishes free of garlic.

Yet, last week, she had slipped. Almost. They had been at a party, one of those wild ones that had dancing and music so loud, and a lot of boozing before dinner would be served after midnight... A waiter had gone past, loftily holding a tray full of Bloody Marys. The salt-edged glasses tinkled in the spotlight, and he had caught sight of the luscious red liquid splashing quietly between the rims, as the tray glided past.

And at the look in his eyes, her heart froze for a moment, then uttered a scream of pure terror; but she had moved nevertheless. And swung gaily past on her partner's arm, bumping into him, upsetting his momentum, for she knew what he was about to do, and could not let it be done. He had let out a wild, wild shriek that chilled the ebullience of the terrace party for a long moment. Then she had made a big fuss, and said, "I'm so sorry, my dear darling, these stilettos can really hurt. But you mustn't flirt so, you know."

And everyone had laughed, and said, "Ah, green-eyed maiden, you clever, clever woman, you stepped in just in time and got your husband back from the brink."

He had indeed got back from the brink; and the moment was saved. But she had learnt another lesson. No tomato juice; no Bloody Marys.

She kept instead tiny platters of blood from the meat she washed in the fridge. A good wife, she knew, must feed her man all his favourite foods. She noted with satisfaction that when the moon was not full, he would sleep quiet and deep by her side, and not roar with an unnamed restlessness.

Then, one day, she cut herself. She was chopping onions, tears were choking her eyes, welling like a flood. For one long moment, she indulged in the release, let it flow, let the dam that held her in burst and carry all emotion, all caution, all feeling with her.

Defences down, she let herself go, and standing over the cutting board, knife in hand, she let her tears flow. Huge salty tears, and not all of them onion induced. Waves of self-pity overwhelmed her. Why, she wondered, did she have to contend with this, why did she have to hide and seek and find only to hide the knowledge again?

She felt then she would have settled for a clerk, a 'babu,' a dimwit, a good-for-nothing, anything, anyone, except her handsome, creative go-getter husband: The marvel of the ad world, the creative genius whose every slogan was a sell-out, whose smile devastated, whose eyes hypnotised and whose wings beat the night when the moon hung full outside her window.

The tears splashed on. She pulled herself short. This wouldn't do, she said to herself, very sternly. After all, what is a bit of night flying between real lovers? Other husbands do worse things, have affairs, swindle their bosses, become impotent. And she set to slicing onions again.

A flutter of wings made her jump, but it was only the crow outside the window looking in, beady-eyed, for scraps. But she had got a start – what a start – and her hand jumped and the knife slipped right over the shiny onion skin, slippery with her tears, and plunged straight into the flesh, pliant and soft and almost waiting, of her thumb.

She stared for a moment in horror, then, almost guiltily, as if to hide a treasure before it could be snatched away, she plunged the thumb into her mouth. The iron sting of blood filled her senses, and she almost retched. But the trick had worked. The bleeding was stilled.

She bandaged the thumb carefully in invisible, skin-coloured band aid. It wouldn't do to let him see.

But he knew. She knew he knew, from the way his nose flared as she served him the onion soup; the way the hair at the nape of his neck seemed to move and rise, then flatten against his skin. Next time, I'll throw away the onions, she thought, ruefully. But it was too late. She knew it was too late.

That night he hunted till early into the morning, but not before he had spent his passion and sent her into a dizzying sleep. Eddies of sleep washed over her; she could barely free herself from the dark, whittling tunnel that sucked her into the whorl of its centre, even as she heard the window swing open and the sound of wing beats.

She'd never have known she was so anaemic if she hadn't got pregnant. A fear clutched her heart as she heard the doctor's words resounding from the far end of the now familiar tunnel. She could not, would not, give birth. She couldn't. The anaemia would not make it safe. All day she knit up excuses, and yet there was nothing that could seem plausible.

By day, she nursed her secret. Guarding it like a jealous dog guards a juicy bone, unable to lose it, unwilling to take it in. She felt it, whatever it was that grew within her, gnawing at her insides. Thrashing its webbed feet, and flailing its clawed hands against the wall of her womb. A shriek rose high-pitched within her, deep in her throat and wound its way through her brain.

But at night, she was strangely calm, as she told him. He smiled and let out a whoop of celebration then swept her into his arms. She thought for a moment he had flown out the window, into the open night, but it was whirling her round and round the room and uttering sounds of pure joy.

She knew then she would have to bear this secret, too. Hold it close within her and nurture it, as she had nurtured her husband's needs, and be a good mother as she had been a good wife. Would always be.

Meanwhile, she had to look after herself. Her cravings would make her walk the house in a wild madness, eating grapes by the kilo one day, munching onions on another. She indulged them all, stopping short only at her sudden need for garlic.

Till one day she could bear it no more. The taste of garlic haunted her memory, the banished herb was like a madness beckoning to her. She could taste the bitter pungency at the back of her throat; smell the golden fragrance of it frying in oil in the moments before she fell asleep. She fought it steadily, she knew it would only bring her and all that was only hers, great harm; but the urge would taunt and invoke and run amok with her control.

She found herself searching the fridge for one long-forgotten root she had hidden there in the early months when she knew not what to expect, and had kept for safety, should she need it. Deeper and deeper into the fridge, her fingers closing over, now the crisp green roundness of a capsicum, now the rugged, mottled roughness of a cauliflower. Then plop, she plunged into a little platter, of blood, of course. And the smell of garlic assailed her nostrils, filling her senses with longing.

She dipped her finger into her mouth. The iron rancidness startled her, yet the clanging ceased. The jangled nerves quietened down. She reached out and, with quiet relish, polished off the platter, like a cat would lick its way through a plate of cream.

There is no room here for a requiem. Suffice to say that on moonlit nights, if you care to look closely through the grill of the house she lives in, the beautiful one with damask and lace curtains, you may as likely as not see

A GOOD WIFE

outlined, for a brief moment, three silhouettes.

Their pointed ears, twitching in anticipation, their eyes sharp and bright, quite belying their lack of vision, their wings readying for flight. A moment, barely, then they are gone, winging their way into the night, out on their hunt for adventure and glory.

Of course, you'll know you imagined it all in the morning. When you ring the bell, she will come down to open the door. Butter knife in hand, for she has been preparing breakfast, you see, it's time for Junior to be off to school. And she has to pack her husband's lunch – he hates eating out. Yet she'll bid you enter and make you comfortable, and chat with you as she goes about her chores. And, feeling a bit foolish, you will leave, your questions unasked, your mind thinking, what a good hostess she is. But of course. A good mother, too.

And she's always been a good wife. A real good wife!

2